Wilful Disregard

Lena Andersson (b. 1970) is a novelist and
columnist for *Dagens Nyheter*, Sweden's largest
morning paper. She lives in Stockholm where she is
considered one of the country's sharpest contemporary
analysts. *Wilful Disregard* is her fifth novel and
won Sweden's prestigious August Prize.

LENA ANDERSSON

Wilful Disregard

a novel about love

Translated by Sarah Death

PICADOR

First published 2015 by Picador

First published in paperback 2016 by Picador
an imprint of Pan Macmillan
20 New Wharf Road, London N1 9RR
Associated companies throughout the world
www.panmacmillan.com

ISBN 978-1-4472-6893-2

Originally published in 2013 as *Egenmäktigt förfarande – en roman om kärlek*
by Natur & Kultur, Stockholm.

1 3 5 7 9 8 6 4 2

A CIP catalogue record for this book is available from the British Library.

Printed and bound by CPI Group (UK) Ltd, Croydon, CR0 4YY

Visit **www.picador.com** to read more about all our books
and to buy them. You will also find features, author interviews and
news of any author events, and you can sign up for e-newsletters
so that you're always first to hear about our new releases.

If a person . . . unlawfully takes and uses or otherwise appropriates something, a sentence . . . shall be imposed for unlawful dispossession. The same shall apply to a person who, without any appropriation, by fitting or breaking a lock or by other means unlawfully disturbs another's possession or by violence or threat of violence prevents another from exercising his right to retain or take something.

Swedish Penal Code: Chapter 8, Section 8

There was a person called Ester Nilsson. She was a poet and essayist with eight slim but densely written publications to her name by the age of thirty-one. Self-willed in tone according to some, playful according to others, but most people had never heard of her.

From the horizons of her own consciousness she perceived reality with devastating precision and lived by the understanding that the world was as she experienced it. Or to be more precise, that people were so constituted as to experience the world as it was, as long as they did not let their attention wander, or lie to themselves. The subjective was the objective, and the objective the subjective. That, at any rate, was what she was trying to prove.

She knew that her quest for an equivalent precision in language was a sort of fixation but she pursued it anyway, since every other ideal made it too easy for those who tried to cheat or evade the intellect; those who were not as scrupulous about how phenomena interacted and how they were represented by language.

And yet she was obliged to acknowledge over and over again that words remained an approximation. As did thought, which although constructed of systematized perceptions and language was not as reliable as it claimed to be.

The dreadful gulf between thought and words, will and expression, reality and unreality, and the things that flourish in that gulf, are what this story is about.

Since realizing at the age of eighteen that life ultimately consisted of dispelling melancholy, and discovering language and ideas all by herself, Ester Nilsson had not felt any sense of unhappiness with life, nor even any normal, everyday depression. She worked steadily at decoding the nature of the world and of human beings. She had pursued her studies in philosophy at the Royal Institute of Technology in Stockholm and since completing her thesis, in which she attempted to bring together the Anglo-Saxon and the French traditions, that is, to apply the minimalism and logic of the analytical school to the Continental school's grander assumptions about life, she had been working as a freelance writer.

From the day she found language and ideas and realized where her mission lay, she renounced expensive living, ate cheaply, was always careful about contraception, only travelled rationally, had never been in debt to the bank or to any private person, and did not get herself into situations that forced her away from what she wanted to spend her time doing: reading, thinking, writing and debating.

She had been living like that for thirteen years, and for more than half that time in a quiet, harmonious relationship with a man who left her in peace while satisfying her physical and mental needs.

Then she got a phone call.

The call came at the beginning of June. The man at the other end asked if she wanted to give a lecture in the last weekend of October about the artist Hugo Rask. He had made his name combining moving images and text in a way that was considered both magnificent and singular. He was also rated highly for his moral fervour in a superficial age. Where others spoke of themselves, he spoke of responsibility and solidarity, as his followers liked to put it.

A thirty-minute lecture, the usual fee.

Ester was at Sankt Eriksplan when she took the call. It was late afternoon and she had the intense glare of the low sun in her eyes. When she got home she proudly announced the assignment to the man she lived with, whose name was Per. Hugo Rask was an artist they had both been watching with great interest.

Summer passed, and part of the autumn. Ester Nilsson's life went on as normal. A few weeks before the appointed date she began a close study of Hugo Rask's work and read everything written by and about him. 'Any artist who fails to engage with society and the vulnerability of the individual in a cruel existence should not style him- or herself an artist,' was one of his frequently quoted assertions.

Ester's lecture was to take place on a Saturday. The Sunday before, she sat down and started writing. She had to start in good time, she knew, in order to get behind the collective language, the accepted thinking that had petrified into commonplace phrases.

Ester Nilsson was intending to write a fabulous address. Hugo Rask would be amazed when he heard her. Every artist, and particularly men of enlightenment like him, was receptive to the power of formulations and their erotic potential.

With every day she devoted to preparing the lecture, her sense of affinity with its subject grew. From feeling respect on *Sunday* she progressed to reverence on *Tuesday* and by about *Thursday* she felt an insistent yearning, which on *Friday* turned into a deep sense of lack.

It turned out that a person could miss someone she had never met, except in her imagination.

What she loved was not so much him as her own creation, and though she had not created him (he existed without her), the words, which were hers, now enveloped and caressed his work, which was himself.

The seminar on Hugo Rask's life and work hitherto began at 1 p.m. on the Saturday. Besides her own lecture there would be an art critic speaking and then a panel on 'The social responsibility of the artist'.

They arranged to assemble fifteen minutes before the event started. The air still had some warmth to it and Ester was wearing a thin grey coat that hung elegantly round her legs as if it were expensive, which it was, but she had bought it in a sale. She draped it over the back of the chair next to hers. When Hugo Rask came into the room, it was that particular chair he chose to pull out and sit on, although there were others vacant. But first he picked up her coat in his hand and moved it to the window seat. His fingers closed round the fabric and the gesture with which he moved the garment was the most sensual she had ever witnessed, at least as far as moving an inanimate object was concerned. There was an absolute kindliness in the delicacy of the touch, the physical incarnation of perfect care.

If you touched objects and fabrics like that, you must carry with you an extraordinary tenderness and sensitivity, Ester Nilsson thought.

During the lecture he sat in the front row, paying close attention. There was intense concentration among the hundred and fifty members of the audience, who had all paid to be there. Afterwards, he came up to Ester beaming and thanked her by taking both her hands in his and kissing her on both cheeks.

'No outsider has ever understood me so profoundly and precisely.'

She felt a rushing and roaring inside her and found it hard to follow the rest of the programme. All she could think about was the gratitude she had seen in his face.

When the event ended at five o'clock she stayed close to him and tried not to look too much as she felt. The artist's son was there, a bearded young man in a woolly hat, direct and spontaneous in his manner. He praised her lecture and said they ought to go for a drink or three. It was the only thing in this world and beyond that Ester Nilsson wanted to do. If she had been able to go for a beer with Hugo Rask that evening, her life would have been perfect.

But she had to get home.

Her brother was visiting from abroad and Ester and her partner were having dinner with him and her father. Her brother only came once a year so she could not cancel.

'Another time perhaps,' said Hugo.

'Any time at all,' Ester said in a muffled voice, trying to hide her emotion.

'Why not drop round to the studio some time and pick up those DVDs you couldn't get hold of?'

'I'll be in touch,' Ester said, sounding even more muffled.

'It really was perceptive, your presentation today. I'm touched.'

'Thank you. It was no more than the truth.'

'The truth,' he said. 'That's what we're both looking for, you and I. Am I right?'

'Indeed you are,' she said.

During dinner with her partner, brother and father, Ester was heavy with longing to be elsewhere. The timbre of her voice revealed what she was feeling, as did the glitter in her eyes. She was aware of it but could change neither the timbre nor the glitter. She only wanted to talk about Hugo Rask and his art, and what had been said during the day. At one point she dismissed the artist and ridiculed him in unnaturally harsh yet somehow intimate terms. That, too, told the attentive all they needed to know. But none of the others round the table was particularly attentive.

She felt very alone and completely exhausted. In the course of a few hours, or since the previous Sunday when she had started to write Hugo Rask into existence within her, or as the result of a long disintegration, Ester had become a stranger to her partner. Her whole self was one huge sense of absence.

She felt she could develop a friendship with Hugo, an elective affinity. The artist would get to know her and Per, and come to dinner with them. They would discuss the big questions and broaden one another's minds through conversation. Nothing would change, it would merely be enriched.

Reality is built one step at a time. She was on the second step.

Two weeks had passed by the time she went to him, one carefully chosen evening. In the course of those weeks she had thought of nothing else. The fact that he had asked her to drop round to the studio for copies of his early works meant she had the right to seek him out. So as not to seem too eager, she waited for as long as she could bear to.

The door was opened by one of Hugo Rask's colleagues, wearing paint-spattered work clothes. Ester gave him a long-winded explanation of her visit. She accounted for something nobody was wondering about to hide something nobody could see. When Hugo's associate finally interpreted her simple request, he told her to wait at the door while he went to get the DVDs. He set off rapidly across the room. Ester had been buoyed up by her yearning for another encounter and the disappointment of missing out on it for such trivial reasons would have been too much for her.

'I was to have a word with him, too,' she announced in an over-loud voice, her skin tingling.

There are moments when presence of mind determines

the future, freighted instants that are then gone and it is all too late. She had to dare and she had to do it right now. Everything depended on these few seconds. The associate hesitated. As part of the team of assistants, his role was to protect his employer and idol. He probably hoped to become an artist himself one day and had sought out the great man to watch and learn.

He asked her to wait and disappeared into the building and up a flight of stairs.

When he came back he looked smaller. Ester was allowed to step inside.

Upstairs, Hugo Rask was sitting with a friend named Dragan Dragović, known as someone with whom Hugo Rask was prepared to debate the state of the world, someone who influenced his thinking and served as his superego – though of course things that Hugo possibly should not have said and thought came out in uncensored form. Everything they debated, Dragan and Hugo, was global and eternal in its compass. Small, everyday topics were not their concern.

Nor were they Ester Nilsson's.

Hugo got to his feet and his whole face lit up when he saw her. He embraced her with evident relish and invited her to sit down. Dragan stayed in his seat, one slim leg crossed over the other, and extended a hand in greeting, though not far enough to spare her from having to move towards him. He wore shoes of black leather with a pattern of perforations and was peering through the smoke rising from his cigarette, which made his expression look both superior and indifferent.

'You're a poet?' he said.

'Yes.'

'Translated?'

'Yes. Not very much. It's no measure of—'

'What are you trying to achieve in your poetry?'

'To make other people see what I've seen.'

Dragan said no more. It was impossible to tell whether her answer had satisfied or dissatisfied him, but in Ester's judgement the answer had proved better than he was expecting and he did not like the fact.

'It was fabulous, what you did last Saturday,' said Hugo.

He seemed in a flutter by comparison with Dragan's bad-tempered immobility.

'What was that?' said Ester.

'Your lecture about me.'

She felt the roar of her pounding pulse and looked at Hugo sitting there, big and tall, full of food, drink and years lived. She loved everything she saw, so much that her insides ached.

'I was up in Leksand for the weekend,' he said.

Ester waited for him to continue.

'I've a house there. By Lake Siljan.'

There was something peculiar about the statement as if he, too, was accounting for something nobody was wondering about to hide something nobody could see, and

Dragan raised one eyebrow accordingly. Ester felt he was talking about Leksand and his house because he wanted to introduce every aspect of himself to her without delay.

She sat on an upright wooden chair but did not take off her down jacket. She had bought it yesterday, when the first cold snap arrived. Her trousers were new as well, dark-blue corduroy; the jacket had matching blue-corduroy detail on the shoulders. It was only when every neuro-transmitter in her brain was running in top gear that she could galvanize herself to buy clothes. Otherwise it was far too meaningless an activity, merely stealing time from the self-imposed task of decoding reality and locating language's most truthful illustration of it. One day she would understand how everything was connected. For now, it came in fragments and pieces.

Hugo Rask nodded appreciatively at the jacket and said how smart it was, not as puffy as other down jackets. She unbuttoned it so as not to get too hot but felt that remov-ing it would be like inviting herself to stay and since that was exactly what she wanted – to stay there for ever – she could not take off the jacket.

At that moment she was incapable of perceiving that it would be normal behaviour to take off a thick down jacket even if only staying for a short time. Mimicking normality is the hardest thing of all. It has a lack of concern that is impossible to imitate. Exaggerations show up and look like stupidity. But attempts to hide feelings do have the advantage that the observer does not know for sure. Taken to extremes, life is a process of reorientation after shame or glory, and when anxiety sweeps in there is a relief at not having left any definite tracks. Having kept a jacket on, having seemed awkward or nervous, these are not proof in the way utterances are proof. At most they are circumstantial evidence.

Ester Nilsson, who generally dismissed shame and glory because both of them made the individual a slave to the judgements of others, now sat there wondering how much or how little she should take her jacket off to ensure nobody noticed how much she was in love.

They talked about Hugo, his works, his stature and achievements. He asked her a little about herself but she swiftly brought the conversation back to him, referring to a sequence of images he had done of people at a bus stop in the rain, which had recurred over the years.

Why that theme, and why recurring?

Hugo got up, stretched his arms in the air, took a few steps and tore down a note that was stuck to the wall. She saw his body from behind and wanted to rush over and hold it.

'Because it's beautiful,' he said, crumpling the slip of paper and throwing it into a waste-paper basket.

She felt weak in every joint at seeing these physical movements and at the sensuality that must reside in anyone who sees that people in the rain can be beautiful. Was this not exactly what she had been seeking all her life?

But she had to go home to a man who was waiting for her, a man so afraid of the answer that he no longer asked where she had been and why she had stopped talking to him.

One afternoon, Ester met a friend at a cafe. They drank coffee and ate American muffins and talked about everything that was happening in their lives. Ester liked her friend a lot; they had known each other for a long time. When they had been chatting for a while, the friend gave Ester a quizzical look and asked:

'Are you in love with Hugo Rask? You blush every time his name comes up. In fact your face is permanently flushed.'

Ester gripped her serviette.

'But I shan't leave Per.'

Her friend went from quizzical to surprised.

'Oh, was that on the cards?'

'No.'

Her friend went from surprised to sympathetic certainty.

'We've made contact at a deep level and we're going to be friends,' said Ester.

Her friend smiled in amusement. But Ester believed what she was saying. She did not realize she had crossed a boundary. The brain knows no tenses. If it has longed for something, it has already had it. The leap comes when we do not want to lose the future we have already known.

'Your face is all red,' said her friend.

Ester raised her hands to her cheeks, mainly to cover them, but also to cool them.

'It's hot in here,' she said.

Passion was raging inside her. Its internal combustion engines were firing on all cylinders. She was living on air. She did not eat but needed no nourishment. She did not drink but felt no thirst. With every passing day her trousers hung more loosely. Her flesh was burning and she could not sleep. She had started putting her mobile in her dressing-table drawer and in the reckless self-absorption of being in love she failed to register that the man beside her was lying awake in silent fury. Despair was too big a word, because he was a reserved type, even to himself, but not many sizes too big.

The implication hitherto had been that Per and Ester liked each other's company and were always together, whereas the implication now was that Ester did not come home in the evenings until she had to. Their whole relationship had been implied, so its disintegration also took place without comment.

Hugo's text messages generally arrived at night, when his assistants and Dragan had gone home and he was still working away on his own. Every evening around midnight he would send a friendly line that she read the instant it arrived. In the bed beside her lay a human being who did not exist.

His studio was on Kommendörsgatan, in one of the few unassuming buildings on the street. In the evenings she would patrol the surrounding area. She hoped to catch a glimpse, hoped that someone in his circle, or even he himself, might emerge from the front door. And one evening, it happened. On her way home from the cinema, she took a detour past his place to do some more circuits of his block. All at once she spotted him on the other side of the street, walking along the pavement. He was heading briskly in the opposite direction. She turned and followed at a distance. He rounded a couple of corners and went into the ICA Esplanad supermarket on Karlavägen. Ester waited outside.

He emerged three and a half minutes later holding a small bag and went back the way he had come. She made sure to stay twenty metres behind. As they approached the entrance to his building, she caught up with him, put her hand on his shoulder and said:

'What a coincidence.'

He expressed no surprise but touched her arm and said:

'Come on up. We're having a chat after work, just me and a few of my associates.'

'Are you sure the others would want me to?'

'I want you to. Do come.'

There were five people standing in the studio's kitchen, their glasses charged with red wine and their elbows propped on the bar counter. He produced what he had bought: crackers, grapes and some blue cheese, which he unwrapped from its plastic packaging.

One of his collaborators, a youngish woman with frizzy hair and startling spectacles, gave Ester a sideways look, but that was presumably a misreading, because Ester saw no reason why she should.

They ate and drank and said how delicious the cheese was. Hugo explained that the taste combination of bread, cheese and grape had taken centuries to develop. Only this extended timescale had allowed them to evolve to appeal perfectly to the taste buds. She loved the fact that he reflected on such big and important topics.

The only thing that dissatisfied her was the fact that he always had people around him. It said something about him that made her feel vaguely sceptical. She would have preferred him to be a solitary being with a fissure of longing in him that she could fill.

Before you understand where the emotion is going to lead, you talk to anyone and everyone about the object of your love. All of a sudden, this stops. By then the ice is already thin and slippery. You realize that every word could expose your infatuation. Feigning indifference is as hard as acting normally, and fundamentally the same thing.

Ester had still not reached that point, which became evident at an event where she ran into the editor of the philosophy periodical *The Cave*, for which she had occasionally written, and immediately turned the conversation to Hugo Rask, although they were talking about something else. The editor agreed that he was extremely interesting, and had a sudden idea. She said they were just putting the finishing touches to an issue on the theme of self-sacrifice and duty but still felt something was missing, something to tie everything together and attract readers at the same time. The editor had not decided what it should be until this moment. As Hugo Rask's work always revolved round ethical issues, the editor proposed an interview with him about the tension between I and You, in his work and for him personally.

Ester Nilsson felt her hair follicles tingle with heat as she asked the editor why she felt Ester was particularly suited to the commission because, after all, she had not addressed those tensions either in her own work or in her study of his.

'Because you're in love with Hugo Rask and will dare to ask questions it would never occur to other people to ask.'

'What makes you think that?'

'Think what?'

'That one would ask penetrating questions in that case.

I thought it was generally considered to be the other way round, namely that being in love makes one uncritical, undiscriminating.'

'Undiscriminating, certainly. But not uncritical; severe, rather. If the object of one's affections proves to be pitiful, contradictory and weak, it simply makes one love them more.'

'It sounds as though you're speaking from experience.'

'You bet I am.'

The editor smiled more broadly than was advisable for someone with a set of teeth ruined by wine and cigarettes.

'But there's another, much more immediate reason for asking you to do it.'

'And what's that?'

'Only someone in love would be able to produce an article like that within the week. I'm afraid that's all the time I can give you.'

'What makes you think I'm in love?'

'I can tell from the way you look.'

'I rate his art highly,' said Ester. 'I genuinely do.'

The editor gave an indulgent and slightly unkind laugh.

'2,500 words maximum, 2,250 minimum. Submission date a week from now.'

An interview of this sort called for hours of conversation and a good deal of contact thereafter, to discuss the framing of the text. This was her chance.

—

The next morning, she called Hugo. He was flattered but wanted to consider the matter, for this was a weighty subject that demanded a lot of time and thought; it had to be right and it had to be good. But in principle he was interested, and he respected *The Cave*.

In the course of that day she discovered the impossibility of telling her partner about the commission and realized their relationship was over. The question that remained was how she was going to say it. She hoped he would help her. And that was indeed what happened. He could not cope with living with the ambivalence and the following evening he gripped her firmly by the top of her arm and said:

'Is there any point in this any longer? In us?'

But behind his words, Ester discerned above all a wish for reassurance and relief. He was saying it to find out that he was wrong. There is a resistance in the party who wants to leave, a fear of the unknown, of the hassle and of changing one's mind. A party not wanting to be left must exploit that resistance. But then they must restrain their need for clarity and honesty. The matter must remain unformulated. A party not wanting to be left must leave it to the one wanting to go to express the change. That is the only way to keep a person who does not want to be with you. Hence the widespread silence in the relationships of the world.

Ester thought: I mustn't. I mustn't soften his pain and my own inconvenience. I mustn't.

'No, there's no point,' she said.

'So it's over?'

'Yes.'

'In that case you can move out tomorrow.'

'I've nowhere to live.'

'When I get home from work tomorrow, I want you to be gone.'

The next morning, she moved back in with her mother in Tulegatan. Her mother asked neither too many questions nor too few. She said Ester could stay as long as she needed to. When she awoke the first morning there was no sorrow, no sense of loss, just a sensation of freedom. Nobody can pretend away their rapture. It is said that breaking up is always hard. But if you are in love with someone else you are not going to be simultaneously sad, not really. You may feel weighed down by guilt and the complications in prospect, you can suffer with the other party. But your love is total, even totalitarian. It envelops everything you do and think, hence its power to inflict damage.

Ester arranged to meet Hugo for the interview the following Sunday at one o'clock.

Sunday was a grey, damp, raw day with half-closed eyes. It was almost 1 p.m. and she was standing in one of the streets that intersected his own, waiting for the moment when she could ring at his door. She was calm at the prospect of the encounter. Concentrated discussion of real things for several hours was something at which she could not fail. Her only vague worry was the thought of missing out on the future in which her desire was already nesting.

She realized she was starving and bought a vegetarian hot dog at the kiosk outside Hotel Mornington in Nybrogatan. She finished eating it on the stroke of one. She waited for a further two minutes. Crossed into his street and walked along to his studio. Rang the doorbell. He opened the door. Gave her a clumsy hug, his gaze shifting uneasily. A new, thin-skinned and slightly shamefaced introspection had penetrated his usual good-natured joviality. The easy-going demeanour of old had deserted him. It was the first time they met each other alone and in his hung-over eyes there was a hazy awareness that anything they were about to undertake would have consequences.

She registered that his underpants appeared to be of

the tighter-fitting type. They each took a chair at the big, solid desk covered in papers and books, switched on the tape recorder and started.

There were many who considered him obsessed with morality in his work, she ventured cautiously, to test the ground and get things going. Or perhaps by human beings and human nature, archetypal human behaviour?

That was the way he would prefer to describe it, he said, apparently appreciating the observation. Obsessed with humanity per se, yes. But obsessed was too negative a word, it was more a case of a detailed interest. The individual differences between people were only of interest to him for the light they shed on the humanity of human beings, which was what he was seeking. He sought the sign for the thing, as in Plato's world of ideas. The human being as a human being. The chair as a chair, the body of all bodies.

This made him hopelessly passé in the eyes of those parts of the intelligentsia that had long since abandoned all forms of universality and human nature, Ester pointed out. The human of all humans could not be designated, they said, without turning out to be a white, European, middle-class man. The chair of all chairs did not exist because it was Western and from a particular era. And the body he spoke of was proto-fascist.

He passed no comment on this but said that the best way of seeking truth, in both art and science, was to force yourself to see things anew, as they were, pared to the bone, and by never assuming them or their forms to be self-evident. If you wanted to observe the movements of a human being, you should look at the skeleton. If you wanted to observe oppression, you should seek out the formula for oppression; any variations were only there to confuse your eyes and everything emanated from a single original phenomenon, both people and things.

Ester said that she entirely shared this view of the unifying principles of existence, the basic structure for everything to exist. The question was precisely how much notice to take of the critique of it.

Ester knew that Hugo was more concerned with how he wanted to come across to the readers than with worrying about whether she shared his view, and it was right that he should be. The fact that she had a secondary agenda for the conversation did not mean he had to. She would be patient and play a long game.

Ester changed tack and asked what he based his morality in, whether he judged actions in terms of consequences or principles. He did not seem to understand the question, upon which she explained that she sometimes reflected on whether we are in fact not all to some extent utilitarians, that is consequentialists, that is, judged things in terms of outcome, even when we claimed to be applying principles.

'What do you mean?' he asked sharply, with an air of irritation. 'There's no contradiction there, is there?'

Ester felt nervous but decided it would be more embarrassing to relinquish her argument than to see it through.

'A consequentialist,' she said, 'is obliged to be against

democracy if it turns out to have worse consequences than dictatorship. For her, there can be no intrinsic value in anything other than maximum well-being, whereas for the rights-based ethicist, intrinsic value is the only orientation point. The intrinsic value of freedom and autonomy.'

After every sentence she paused for a moment, but no response came.

'What the rights-based ethicist then has to endure is the thought that her stance could have worse consequences than other stances, whilst still standing by and being able to justify the principle of the individual's freedom and autonomy.'

Hugo's face was expressionless except for a vague questioning look. Even absence of expression is an expression, noted Ester.

'So how does the rights-based ethicist deal with that?' she ploughed on, regretting the whole digression. 'Isn't it still the case that in the long run, the rights-based ethicist believes that the autonomy of the individual is the only thing that can produce acceptable consequences? And thus inevitably lands up in consequentialism, a form of rule utilitarianism?'

Hugo, his hands on the arms of his chair, rocked thoughtfully back and forth.

'In the long run we're all dead, as Keynes put it,' he said.

'And how do intrinsic values and principles arise in any case?' said Ester. 'That is, those things which the utilitarian shuns but on which the rights ethicist bases her whole approach? Isn't it of necessity, by comparison with alternatives, presumed to be worse? But worse compared to what? Surely it has to be the outcome, entirely discounted by the rights-based ethicist, that is the point of comparison?'

Hugo's eyes had started to wander. He said:

'When they asked Zhou Enlai about the effects of the French Revolution almost two hundred years after it happened, do you know what his answer was? "Too early to say." Isn't that wonderful? "Too early to say." '

Hugo gave a sudden laugh. It was not of the inclusive variety.

'But with perspectives that long we're all dead, as you say,' said Ester.

'I'm an artist,' said Hugo. 'There's a morality in aesthetics too.'

'Tell me more.'

He said: 'Aesthetics is a moral act.'

She said: 'What does that mean?'

He said: 'It means that aesthetics, art per se, has revolutionary power.'

She said: 'Regardless of content?'

He said: 'If it hasn't, then it's not art.'

She said: 'So is that a definition?'

He nodded. She asked what the rest of it was, then, the stuff which was called art but wasn't, because it lacked revolutionary power.

He said: 'Crafts. Or rubbish.'

They moved on to talk about details of his work. She

toned down the subject of the interview, I and You, as his answers turned out to consist mainly of impenetrable quotations or accounts of Buber. When they ranged more widely Hugo expounded on his text each time as though no question had been asked, and each time he appropriated the wording of the question as his own. Ester got the feeling she was providing the words for what he was engaged in and who he was, but that he simultaneously believed he was the one thinking them.

After three hours she thought she had what she needed to put together an article and turned off the tape recorder. Her head felt really tired and she looked at her watch. It was too early for dinner.

They sat and rested for a while and chatted of other things, small talk about a lovely violin that hung on his wall and about what was going on in the street below, which they observed as they got to their feet and stood beside each other at the window. She craved his body. She happened to mention that her own relationship had come to an end and that she was living with her mother while waiting for a flat. He fiddled with his paper clips and looked as though he wanted to suggest something. Ester said she planned not to start writing the article until first thing the following morning when her brain felt refreshed. Now it was jaded and tired.

'Are you hungry?' asked Hugo.

'Yes.'

'Me too.'

'I only had a hot dog for lunch, just before I came here. A vegetarian one from the hot-dog kiosk down by the hotel.'

'They have good hot dogs there.'

'I've read about it in the newspaper,' said Ester. 'It's quite famous, isn't it?'

'But I don't eat much in the way of hot dogs. Do you?'

'No. I hardly ever eat hot dogs.'

'So there's such a thing as a vegetarian hot dog? I had no idea. What are they made of?'

'Vegetable matter, processed and compressed into a skin. It's not exactly healthy but perhaps better than meat.'

'Nutritionally?'

'Yes. And morally.'

'Better in utilitarian terms?' he said and gave a warm, gentle laugh. 'Or from a rights-based ethical standpoint?'

So he had been paying attention to what she said, after all.

'I've taken up jogging again,' he said. 'This past week. But I immediately started to feel a strain in the inside of my knee.'

Ester thought he must have started jogging because he had noticed her looking at his body and loving him.

'It could be your meniscus. Can I feel it?'

He extended his knee and she prodded it for a long time.

'A few years ago I could jog pretty well. I'd like to start again. Perhaps we could jog together?'

'As long as this isn't some kind of injury.'

'But you're sure to run faster than I do.'

'We'll decide together how fast we're going to run,' said Ester.

He bent and stretched his leg a few times and said:

'Mmm, aha, yes. So you don't eat many frankfurters. What do you eat, then?'

'Plants, mostly.'

'Plants?'

'And a prawn every now and then.'

'Why plants?'

'Because I can't find any way to defend the eating of conscious life forms. And it may also prolong our lives.'

'How long do you want to live?'

'To around a hundred.'

'That sounds a long time. Don't you think it might get a bit tedious towards the end?'

'No. It all depends on what you're doing.'

He looked out of the window at the restaurant on the other side of the street. His usual haunt.

'If you're not in a hurry we could go and eat a few plants and talk over whether we've covered everything in our interview. The really interesting things often crop up afterwards.'

'You've already said lots of very interesting things.'

He looked at her in a different way from before, with a sort of imploring intensity, and said:

'Do you think so? Do you think I had some decent points to make?'

'You certainly did. Obviously you say interesting things.'

She got the impression there was something weighing on him that he wanted to express and then hear her honest opinion, but preferably her corroboration.

'For me it's not obvious at all,' he said. 'I hear people say it sometimes but that's not how it feels to me.'

'Everyone knows and thinks you're interesting. If anybody does express criticism, they do it in the knowledge of your eminence.'

'Do you think so?'

'I know so.'

She had put on her coat and hat.

'How do you know?' he insisted.

'They find you interesting in the same way that I do.' The words grated slightly inside her.

They would not have long to wait for the restaurant to open at five. In the meantime, he showed her books that had been important for the development of his ideas. In her heart of hearts she was not all that impressed by his ideas but his art was headstrong and the fact that she was in love lent even his ideas a certain sheen.

He had two copies of Camus's *The Rebel* and gave her one of them, the one that had been looked after better and had a cover similar to that of the original, or at least to the way she assumed the original must have looked. It was French in a sallow sort of way, with a rectangle of red lines.

'Camus has been important to me,' said Hugo.

'Camus is wonderful,' said Ester. 'I shall never forget how I felt when I read *The Outsider*. The style, the tone, the opening sentence. The economy of expression.'

'Once upon a time I knew that whole page off by heart in French,' said Hugo.

'Why?'

Hugo was away with Camus now and gave an introspective smile.

Ester said:

'Do you remember that dreadful sequence where his girlfriend asks if he loves her? And he replies that it's immaterial.'

Hugo never followed up anything Ester said. Ester always followed up what Hugo said. Neither of them was really interested in her but they were both interested in him.

Ester made an internal note of his lack of curiosity and generosity, but did not let it influence the reverence she felt.

On the dot of five they went across the road to eat. They talked non-stop until ten o'clock, when they finished off the last of the wine. She thought that if they could keep a conversation going from 1p.m. to 10p.m., there was nothing to worry about. It meant the future was bright.

In the week that followed, Ester worked on the article for *The Cave*. She did it in the same heady state as, in what felt like another time entirely, she had written her lecture about him a month before.

Texts seek their own rhythm. It takes time. But at a certain point, a piece of writing is finished even for a person prepared to work on it indefinitely. This happens when it has become so distanced from the original idea that every reading comes as a surprise and the clarity comes spilling out.

She worked on the interview for more hours a day than she was generally capable of. She normally found extended bouts of writing too much for her. After a certain number of hours, her brain did nothing but querulously identify errors – the deletion of which she regretted the next day – or regurgitate hackneyed phrases.

Eight days after she received the commission, the long article had been completed, read by Hugo, discussed by the two of them in the company of Dragan Dragović, who criticized most of its content and displayed signs of jealousy in a variety of other ways, and submitted to the editorial team. They replied that they were happy with it and asked how she had produced it in such a short time.

'Well, I had a deadline.'

'But that's extremely quick work.'

'Were you expecting an inferior article or did you think I wouldn't meet the deadline?'

'What do you mean? We're happy. It's good.'

'Thanks. I'm glad. But surely your editors can't go around handing out commissions they consider impossible?'

'I don't know what you're talking about. Send in your invoice.'

With work on the article over, Ester and Hugo carried on seeing each other at least one evening a week. They had dinner at the restaurant, their conversation was inexhaustible, and afterwards he almost always invited her up to the studio, where they went on talking, but never to his flat, which was in the same building but on the other side of the courtyard. She wondered why nothing was happening. They seemed to be marking time, though the direction was clear enough. She despaired at the thought that it might amount to no more than this and asked him in a text message: 'Can't you say something about how you feel?' He replied with an aphorism, sufficiently cryptic not to put him under any obligation. 'A human is a joy to another human.' She thought dismally: 'A human is a wolf to another human.'

She wondered whether it had been utter madness for

her, neither reflecting nor agonizing and propelled purely by emotions, to leave a well-functioning relationship in order to step out into this void. The fact was that she shunned ennui, always had done. She would rather endure torment than tedium, would rather be alone than in a group of people making small talk. Not because she disliked the small-talkers, but because they absorbed too much energy. Small talk drained her. Perhaps, she debated with herself, she had engineered falling in love with Hugo because she had imperceptibly grown bored and needed this anxiety intermingled with hope and a bliss that was absolute, in order to feel alive.

But now the very air she breathed seemed alarmingly desolate.

There was something holding him back. Perhaps there were unknown obstacles. It struck her that the phenomenon of *no just cause or impediment to marriage* must have arisen to dispel precisely such qualms. She had thought of it as a meaningless concept from an irrational age. But presumably it was to avoid exactly this sort of situation that the question had existed. The strict rules then governing life together were in actual fact far more rational, in the sense of being properly planned and thought out, than this idiocy of caprice and sentiment into which she had thrown herself and to which all modern-day people were consigned. No rules, no traditions, no crutches to lean on, nothing.

She could not comprehend how she would live through

it if this were to end in any way other than their becoming lovers, mutually agreeing that they belonged together.

Every other weekend, Hugo went away. He said he was going to Borås, where his frail mother lived, but there was something about these trips to Borås that did not quite add up. There was an unusual vacuum around them, the way unusual vacuums usually surround lies. The baffling thing was that there was no reason to doubt that the trips were genuine, in the same way that there was no reason he should name a place where he was not going. But there was still something not quite right.

On one of the evenings when they met over food and wine and then went back to his studio, she saw a train ticket sticking out of the inside pocket of his jacket, which was hanging on the back of a chair. When he went to the toilet she got up and walked round the room, looked at the art works on the walls and gave the ticket a slight tweak, so light that it hardly counted as an act.

The ticket was from the previous weekend. Stockholm–Malmö return, it said. Not a hint of Borås.

Once she had recovered she told herself that it was good news. The fact that he was keeping quiet about his long-distance relationship, for that must be what he had in Malmö, indicated that it was winding down and there was a good chance he would make a change.

A few days before Christmas Eve, Ester texted Hugo to ask if she could drop by with a Christmas present. He replied that he was taking the night train to Malmö-Copenhagen that night but she was welcome to pop in for a while before he left for the station. Something had now prompted him to give the correct geographical location, albeit with an attempt to make it more diffuse by the addition of Copenhagen, or to make it sound more interesting and metropolitan.

Ester thought this new honesty must spring from a feeling of greater closeness. If you were close, you did not want to lie. Lying demands a certain amount of dehumanization, at least at that moment. Lying is a carapace. Not to lie when the temptation exists is to render oneself naked.

There were banks of snow in the centre of Stockholm and icicles hung from the roofs. Happily anticipating their short encounter but uneasy about the weeks of Christmas ahead and the uncertain future, she picked her way along the slippery pavements with her Christmas present.

He offered her some red wine although it was barely five. The conversation flowed easily. Their words were welding sparks and attended by weightless laughs. She felt at home, comfortable and content. It was with him she wanted to be, anywhere in the world as long as it was with him.

His suitcase was packed and ready. She gave him her present, carefully chosen and purchased at the second-hand bookshop.

'Is it good?' he asked when he had opened the parcel to reveal the novel *Maj: A Love Story* by Jan Myrdal.

'Outstanding,' said Ester.

'Myrdal's important,' he said. 'An important thinker.'

'I perhaps wouldn't recommend him as a thinker,' said Ester. 'But his language is extraordinarily effective and he's clear-sighted on questions of the human heart without ever getting syrupy or soft. How can one portray a human being from the inside in language or imagery without the transmission process introducing a false note? That's the question. Metaphorizing feelings can only lead away from those feelings. With Myrdal, one feels what they experience as if one were experiencing it oneself.'

'Feelings are something one should be wary of portraying,' said Hugo. 'I mean, it's all about manipulating the recipient into feeling what you want them to feel. That isn't achieved by showing the feelings in question, but by evoking them. Which calls for entirely different means.'

Ester said:

'I think the basic problem is that we interpret others' actions in behaviourist terms, objectively and from the outside. We interpret our own in phenomenological terms, from within our own consciousness. That's the human dilemma. And that's why we all have such extensive understanding of our own actions and so little of others'.'

He refilled her glass and then his own, and said:

'Isn't it more the opposite: people are terribly self-critical, too quick to understand others while condemning themselves?'

'You think so? It's not something I've noticed, I must say.'

'Oh?'

'Or at least, only as a flattering veneer, compensation for the aggression we feel towards other people. But in this book, Myrdal actually succeeds in being both phenome-nological and behaviourist without letting us see how he does it.'

He gave her a benign look, with a cautious kind of smile.

'You think that is its mystique?'

Ester felt embarrassed. She loved him so much that it hurt all over.

'How long will you be away?' she said.

'About two weeks.'

'That's a long time.'

He remained silent, hesitated, was on the verge of saying something but stopped himself.

'Just at the moment I don't know whether I'm coming or going. I simply don't know. I might go up to Leksand for a bit, too.'

'Leksand. To your house?'

'I go there when I want to be on my own and think.'

He turned away and started fiddling with something in a cupboard, restless movements with no purpose. She thought he had just sent her a veiled enquiry, a covert question about whether it would be safe for him to make the break from his woman, the one he was possibly going to see in Malmö. Would Ester be there for him, if he did? Was he asking, with his 'don't know whether I'm coming or going', whether he could trust her or whether she was toying with him? Was he in fact the one who felt vulnerable and not the other way round? It had not occurred to her until now.

She gave him a seasonal peck on the cheek and left, levitating through the streets among the crowds of Christmas shoppers.

She told her mother none of this. Her mother would have thought it unseemly. A little decorum was required, none of this throwing oneself from one thing to another. It was particularly important to leave 'attached men' alone. Admittedly all the indications until very recently had been that Hugo was a free man. There had not been the slightest trace of a liaison except for that train ticket, the strange weekend trips and the vacuum surrounding them.

It was a quiet Christmas. She read *The Rebel*. It was so difficult that she read each sentence twice. Camus wrote it in protest against Sartre's revolutionary totalitarianism, a protest that interested her. When a week had passed she could no longer restrain herself and sent a text: 'Reading

Camus. Revolution is incompatible with the functioning of the human brain. That is, with being human. We cannot deal with the inherent absolutism and abruptness of revolution. Everything a human does is gradual. All her insights, all her thoughts, everything that happens and is said is part of a process, layer upon layer of experience gained. Life itself is lived gradually, by definition, and consciousness is created that way, by evolution. We are drawn to love in order to feel that someone is seeing us.'

She immediately realized that the last sentence was superfluous and high-flown, and out of place. But it was too late; the message had been sent.

No reply was forthcoming, only a crushing anxiety. It intensified as day succeeded day and she heard nothing from him. Her shame at having exposed herself and received no response completely ruined what remained of the holiday period, eating further and further into her nerves. She could not concentrate, told herself to give up, never to care about him or anyone else again, because she could not go on like this. She did not want him! He would be banished from her life!

After the New Year, he was back in Stockholm. She received an email the same day. 'I'm back now. If we work well today, we can reward ourselves with dinner tonight.'

Two short sentences and all her anxiety evaporated. She

worked willingly all through the day. Then she went to the gym, cycled, ran, showered and made herself look nice. On her way to see him she went into a hotel bar for a drink. She had never done anything like that before. Dressed in a casually elegant pair of trousers, blouse and jacket, she sat in an armchair and had a gin and tonic while she finished reading *The Rebel*. From the bar she sent a friend a text in which she described the situation and said she felt she was growing up. It was a foolish phrase and a foolish idea, she sensed, but it introduced some poetry into the experience. She thought as she sat there, sipping a drink in a hotel bar and reading a French classic, that these so-called follies existed because they most exactly mirrored a certain type of feeling.

His round face was glowing with delight as she entered his studio on the dot of six. He smelled nice, was freshly shaven, had damp, neatly combed hair and was wearing cleaner, smarter clothes than he normally did.

'Are you hungry?' he asked, beaming.

She was hungry.

'Let's go then.'

And they went. That evening to the more up-market Sturehof.

Dragan Dragović and the assistants had vanished and were no longer on the premises when they went back to his studio after their restaurant sessions. But nothing happened. Even though their conversations were so erotically charged that anyone who saw them would have received an electric shock, their evenings ended with a chaste kiss and her meek journey home through the night.

Ester tried to think that the slow pace meant it was beautiful. Anything important takes time, she thought. When both are equally eager it takes longer, she had read. This was a prelude of the kind that one could tell others about later because it was so beautiful and tender, she thought, going almost mad with the slowness of it. She would have exchanged all the ethereal sensitivity in the world for a chance to get started on their life together. There were days when she felt the cold draught of impending disaster. There are always reasons why people do things or don't, she thought. Something must lie behind his passivity. If he wanted to be with her more than this, he would be.

Because she was standing in a heavy bog and getting nowhere even when she squelched around in it, there was no way of freeing herself. She hazily recollected that until recently she had devoted herself to matters other than her feelings, taken an interest in the outside world, tried to learn things and enjoyed the sheer fact of her existence. Now all she did was try to understand whether he wanted her or not.

She longed for the clarity that only physical consummation can bring. She wanted the two of them to fuse so that

LENA ANDERSSON

they could then become accessible to each other, be permitted certain expectations.

In a state of constant arousal she caressed herself into short-lived, futile pleasure. Her aching heart, her desire for a body, a skin and a pair of embracing arms could not be relieved by masturbation.

A few weeks into January, the housing department offered her an apartment. She had been in the queue just long enough, since her eighteenth birthday, to qualify for a bedsit in the centre of town. It was in Sankt Göransgatan, in a peaceful location looking onto a courtyard. She could move in straight away.

Supper was 'his treat' each time they met. A main course and dessert to follow, and a sweet wine with it. Occasionally she would pay, for a less extravagant meal. Between times they were in touch every day. Little thoughts, observations and other bits of nonsense exchanged by email or text message. Every other weekend there would be silence. She did not ask. He mentioned neither Borås nor Malmö-Copenhagen.

She felt they had mortgaged their futures neurologically. That they were now so much a part of each other's consciousness that they could not contemplate losing a future so vividly imagined. She feared, however, that this might not apply to his neurons. Great distress awaited her, in that case. And he was still saying nothing about what they were doing, where it would lead. She knew that the brain would rather retain what it has than master something new. It was built into the structure of the brain and fostered by evolution. The question was, which of the two did he not want to lose? Which of his women – she still assumed he was meeting someone in or near Malmö – was the horror of loss cradling in its protective arms?

One of those evenings when they stayed at the restaurant until it closed and then stood talking in the kitchen in his studio, he broke the pattern of their passivity for the first time and said:

'So what shall we do now?'

She was too nervous to hear that it was not a question but an invitation.

'What do you mean?' she said, thus killing what he had tried to bring about.

'We'll carry on talking the way we always do, presumably.'

'Yes. Presumably we will.'

Silence ensued and then she said:

'You could show me your flat.'

But it was too late. She had muddied the waters too thoroughly.

'You can see that another time, but not now,' he said tersely and dismissively. 'It needs clearing up.'

'You'll have to see my flat as well. I moved in on Thursday.'

'Perhaps. I've got to get to bed now.'

She walked home, mortified. I catch on too slowly and rely on talk when action is what's called for, she thought, feeling utterly desperate. She knew that words were her shield and the screen she ran to hide behind. She also knew that words did not solve everything, even though she considered that they ought to. A touch of verbal awkwardness would have been to her advantage sexually. Then her body would have been obliged to do some work, too. Now words would have to compensate, as always. Words were simpler, more attainable.

Her agony was acute for several days. She lay on the floor in her new apartment, whimpering.

She heard nothing. A week passed. The anxiety and self-reproach made her intensely queasy. The girlfriend chorus told her an opportunity is not that easily lost. If this were worth anything, he would still be there. She had done nothing wrong and he could take the initiative, too, it was not always up to her. The girlfriend chorus comprised the collective good advice and exhortations of her dearest friends. They helped her to endure for a few more hours when the blackness descended like a shroud on life itself.

On the Monday evening of the following week, Hugo was due to give a lecture on the eye's perception of colours. She had known about this for a long time and he had asked her to come. One of his major interests was colour and perception, and how the human eye discerns nuances of shade. It was not her area but his lecture took such a pedagogical approach that she understood what he was saying and felt she had learned something.

Once he had finished speaking and taken the applause, they waved and nodded shyly to each other. She stayed in the background while the audience flocked around him. When he had not disentangled himself after ten minutes, she forced herself to leave the building. They had not arranged to meet afterwards and she did not want to expose herself to the answer that he was not available. She must show her independence even at the cost of a missed encounter. She must not be the obedient dog that she felt like. A behaviouristically autonomous dog, albeit phenomenological.

The lecture had been held in a school on Banérgatan. She walked as slowly as she could towards Karlavägen to get to the underground. Or the bus. Or anything. She hoped he would catch sight of her when he came out of the front entrance and hurry to catch her up.

She reached the crossroads and turned cautiously to look back. He had not yet emerged. On this street corner the evening was to be decided, she knew, and perhaps their future life, since every meeting could be decisive. Once she went round that corner he could no longer see her and the opportunity of spending the evening together would be lost.

Now she was out of sight. Now it was too late. She went for a prowl, circling the block so she came back to the same corner again. She rounded it for a second time and thought that she could not do another circuit in anticipation of his arrival.

At that moment she heard his voice. He called her name, looked both ways for cars before venturing into the road and cut across on the diagonal, walking fast. Even in the dark, broken up by street lights and snow, she could see his big, warm smile.

'You weren't going, were you?'

'No. Well yes. I was on my way home.'

'I got stuck with some of the audience. They wanted my view of one thing and another. One has to be pleasant to people who take an interest. What did you think of the lecture? Was it OK?'

He frowned doubtfully, as he did when he was seeking confirmation but also worrying that his contribution had been weak. She praised his lecture in well-rounded sentences with plenty of content-rich bolstering. It seemed to make him happy.

'Shall we go for a bite to eat?' he said.

'Aren't you going to work? You generally work late.'

She wanted this so much that she felt she had to make him these offers of freedom. They could easily have been interpreted as a polite brush-off. The fact that he did not view them as such meant he must have felt confident of her feelings.

'Haven't I done my bit with the lecture?' he said. 'I thought I'd finished work for the evening.'

'Yes, of course you have.'

'Don't you ever relax?'

His tone was jocular and gentle. Ester felt light-headed and giddy and said:

'Oh, all the time. I'll do anything.'

They hunted round for a bit and ended up at a little

local restaurant on a side street that crossed Kommendörs-gatan. There was a buzz of chatter inside and the windows were steamed up; the volume of the other diners was low enough for them to talk but loud enough for no one to eavesdrop. The decor felt warm compared to the frost outside. There were no free tables but he knew the owner, or perhaps the staff recognized him, and all of a sudden a table for two stood ready, with thick drinking glasses and the cutlery in a ceramic pot; it was that sort of place, down to earth.

She perceived them now, and this evening in particular, as entirely equal in their will to be together. The distanced laughs and amused facetiousness were gone. All evasiveness was gone. He wanted something of her. He had moules frites, she had scampi.

'You once told me you mainly ate plants,' he said. 'But I see you eating animals all the time.'

'Only invertebrates. It's hard to restrict yourself to plants when you're eating out.'

'But there are always plant options, aren't there?'

'Drowned in cream, milk and eggs. That amounts to the same as eating animals. But I think of shellfish as almost like a plant. A marine plant.'

'Perhaps I ought to go in for plants, too,' he said.

'I think so.'

'Or for only eating invertebrates. But why is someone more worthy of protection just because they have a backbone?'

52

He had a crack in his lower lip with a thin streak of dried blood. The crack widened as he smiled. It looked rather painful. When she got to her feet to hang up her coat, which had slipped off its hanger, she could feel him following her body with his eyes and how much she liked it.

Between the main course and the dessert he looked at her and said:

'When shall we have that dinner at your place? So I can see your new apartment.'

She gripped her glass, not the stem but the bowl, with both hands and drank some of the wine in order to be utterly present with all her senses at this moment of break-through, so as not to sabotage it all again with her words and impetuosity.

'How about Saturday?' he said.

'But I've only got one chair,' she said, and was struck at the same instant by the realization that this was not the sort of thing you had to say aloud simply because the thought popped into your head.

'We'll take it in turns to sit on it,' he said.

The split in his lip opened again.

He reached out his hand and stroked her hair.

Then Saturday came. It was early February and the drips from the roofs were just starting to question their future as icicles. Ester had not gone out to buy a chair, but she had a stool that she could sit on while they ate. It was uncomfortable but it would do. After all, they would be lying rather than sitting. They had done enough sitting on chairs. She was washed out by all the expectation but blissfully happy in every pore.

She had just added the grated Gruyère to the sauce, which also contained crème fraiche, white wine, paprika and the pan juices from frying the chicken – the plant kingdom would be left in peace tonight – when he called, at quarter to seven. It did not occur to her that he might be going to cancel. Confidence had still not deserted her.

The nervousness in his voice and actions made her calm, almost reckless.

'I'm here at a taxi rank with a chair,' he said.

'Is it cold?'

'Yes?'

'Is the chair freezing?'

'No, because I've given it a blanket.'

'What about you?'

'I haven't got a blanket.'

'So you're freezing?'

'I'm shaking. But not with cold.'

'Because you're coming to see me?'

'Yes.'

'You need never be nervous of me.'

'Are you sure about that?'

'We've met each other so often.'

'But not in the presence of a chair.'

'Get here as soon as you can. The sauce is waiting.'

As they were talking she stirred the sauce and poured it over the chicken fillets. Now the whole thing had to go in the oven for fifteen minutes, the time it would take him to get to her.

When you love and someone receives that love, the body feels light. When the opposite happens, one kilo weighs three. Love that is just beginning is like dancing on a finely honed edge. It can happen that a kilo never regains its proper weight, which generates a degree of apprehension in the fearful, the experienced and the far-sighted. And in those who do not have Ester's extraordinary capacity for hope.

Ester had bought something with which she was not familiar in order to mix a dry martini. She had heard that this could be drunk before the meal when you had guests and she thought they ought to do so to mark the particularly special nature of this dinner. She could hear that her voice was shrill with embarrassment as she introduced the aperitif. He was not impressed and she felt more stupid still as she sensed that he thought she was being pretentious. He held his glass awkwardly as she showed him round her new lair, which took ten uncomfortable seconds. He made no comment on the apartment and seemed to be wondering why he was being shown it.

They sat down at the table and ate her chicken in a cream and Gruyère sauce with rice and green salad. He praised it all but not enough and she detected ironic overtones in his appreciation of the chicken dish.

'This has got a backbone,' he said.

'I made an exception tonight.'

'And why was that?'

After the chicken they moved to the sofa in front of the television, where they had two sorts of ice cream from an Italian ice-cream parlour, chocolate stracciatella and zabaglione, and with it some Italian biscuits called cantucci, and black coffee that was also Italian. Much like his attitude to her aperitif, he now seemed indifferent to her carefully composed dessert. She would have liked him to be as fond as she was of the heavenly kingdom of desserts, their rich fullness, their palate-filling consistencies which made her eat them with her eyes closed. She had wanted to meet a man who could share that with her. But Hugo was more preoccupied with alcohol.

She had to make do with his politely sampling both sorts of ice cream and helping himself to two cantucci.

They watched the Winter Olympics, which had just started. This evening they were showing the first skiing race, the men's thirty kilometres. He appeared to treat this, too, with a degree of disengagement and bemusement, as if he wondered how anyone could expect him to want to watch skiing on television. And one might indeed think it rather strange, but in view of the fact that their conversation during dinner had been somewhat absent-minded (which had never happened before), they needed something to occupy them. She also wanted to usher normal life into their relationship. They could not sit in restaurants all their lives, looking into each other's eyes and conversing. At some stage they would have to start watching television together as well. But he appeared to be in a constant state of doubt as to what he was doing there. She, too, wondered why he had come when everything they did, ate and said appeared immaterial to him. Or was he in fact insecure, nervous even, on foreign territory where he had no control over what happened? Until now they had always been on his stamping ground, in his venues and haunts, among his associates and in his world.

Once an hour he went to the window for a smoke. Every time she stood beside him, leaning out into the winter night. They talked quietly while the glowing point consumed the cigarette. At the window, the conversation flowed more easily.

The stars sparkled impatiently, almost insistently. With every cigarette break she edged a little closer. Hugo said he ought to give up, and he didn't really smoke anyway. Ester thought really was a strange word. How could you not *really* be doing things and yet be busily doing them? She wanted to touch his body. She wondered whether he was planning to stay the night after they made love or whether he would go home, however late it was.

The fifth cigarette of the evening looked like all the others though their legs were touching, but it was the last cigarette before they went to bed and allowed their bodies to be united.

She thought five cigarettes was a lot for someone who did not really smoke. She thought about the illnesses the cigarettes would give him and how awful it would be to worry constantly about these from that imminent day when they started living together. But by her love she would make him stop smoking.

He seemed uneasy and restrained. She was baffled. Naturally she had protection, otherwise she would not have let him in. But of course he did not know how much she valued freedom, even though she felt she had spoken of little else, one way and another.

'We've got to be careful,' he said, resisting as she moved more urgently.

She stopped in mid-movement.

'Why?'

'So you don't get pregnant.'

'You can rest assured I won't do that. I don't want any children. I want adult love alone. Love that's equal and linear, not vertical.'

His mouth twitched slightly at the high-flown phrases. But to her surprise she also heard a vague disappointment and a new ring in his voice. What she heard was a man's dissatisfaction with not producing in a woman the longing for a child, thus making her into a real woman, a mother. The conditioned disappointment of the male.

Ester and Hugo woke at dawn. They made love again, more restfully now that she was less nervous and he knew that his seed would not grow into a new life.

The sky, violet with splashes of orange, spoke of a cold and beautiful day. The drips from the roof had resumed their previous incarnation as icicles.

Then the morning's conversation began, maybe one of the more common among post-coital interchanges. Its themes were evolutionary: dependence, power, weakness, strength, supply and demand, all expressed in the guise of breakfast.

She said: 'What do you want for breakfast?'

He said: 'I don't want breakfast. I'm going home.'

'But I've got all sorts of things here. Muesli, yogurt, fruit, nice bread, jam and cheese and so on, coffee.'

'I must work.'

'So must I. I work every day, the same as you. But one still has to have breakfast.'

'I'll have something when I get home.'

'You might as well have it here. Then you can start work as soon as you get there. You won't lose any time that way.'

'I don't eat much breakfast. It's not important.'

It's important to me, she thought.

'Breakfast is sort of more than just the eating,' she said.

'Breakfast is energy to see you though to lunch,' he said.

She could tell he wanted to get away. So there was no persuasion left in her words when she said:

'No. It's more than energy. And that's precisely why you're in such a hurry to go.'

No persuasion, and that made it sound like bitterness even though the tone was matter-of-fact. He looked as though he was wondering what to answer.

'Let's be in touch later,' he said cautiously.

'Only if you feel like it.'

'Or if you feel like it.'

'No, I'm afraid that's not how it works. It's if you feel like it that we'll be in touch.'

He dashed out after a quick, harassed kiss.

The door slammed behind him and several combinations of words floated into her mind: *The breakfast fibres squeeze their way through the intestine. Columns of consummate crap. Lovers' tryst adrift.*

She did not like the censure she had allowed herself, the self-pitying passive-aggressiveness, the tone of rejection which, she knew, kills all desire and delight the other person might feel by the sense of guilt it engenders in them. Yet still she had been unable to stop her feelings escaping. She detested it when blame came hissing out like that. She had done so since childhood and had decided never to be like that. And yet she had failed to stop herself venting it when it mattered most.

Prime Minister Tage Erlander (in office 1946–1969) famously described a modernist social structure, also known as the welfare state, as an addiction. That was not what he said, but that was the gist of what he said when he spoke of the dissatisfaction of rising expectations, a psychological law of nature. You got what you had been lacking and were grateful for a brief moment. But you soon adjusted to it, considered it the norm and started to view it as a minimum standard. Your expectations grew and it took more and more to produce the feeling of satisfaction. Running water, nutritious food, a car and more spacious housing were not enough. Bigger, more sweeping reforms were needed to make you feel as good as you had before. The dose had to be higher and be administered more frequently.

Ester was not happy despite the union of their flesh. She did not think he had made his intentions clear. She was anxious about what would happen next.

After breakfast on that first morning of their new phase she went out and ran fifteen kilometres. She was training for the Stockholm marathon and did one long-distance run every week. She did this on Sundays. As an amateur on the periphery of a community she did the same as everybody else, and everything the advice columns urged her to. Marathon runners did one long run a week, generally on Sundays because most of them were at work during the week. She could do her own training run any day she liked but she, too, chose Sundays. Later in the spring she intended to increase the distance to twenty kilometres, heeding the advice, but fifteen was enough for now. Ambition levels had to be balanced against the risk of injury.

When she got home she hurtled to the telephone without even waiting to take her shoes off. No messages. He had neither called nor sent a text. For her suffering not to become acute, the liquid level of love needed constant topping-up.

Her emotional life was now subject to the dissatisfaction of rising expectations. The only advantage of this is that after a time, the disappointment can turn into another law of nature, namely the delight that sinking expectations take in the tiniest positive detail.

But the poison was in him, too. He rang that afternoon. The call came from a landline number she did not recognize. He had lost his mobile phone, he told her, or rather, left it on the back seat on his way home that morning. The taxi firm had promised to return it to him as soon as they had a driver coming that way. He was so eager to be in touch, she thought, the exhilaration fizzing in her breast, that he had taken the trouble to look up her number so he could ring her that very same day, on no particular pretext. He sounded uncomfortable and that particularly pleased her. Could it be the case, she thought, that his absent-mindedness in mislaying his phone was the result of feeling punch-drunk?

They told each other what a wonderful night it had been. She told him about her training run and how easy it had been, because you weigh so little when you are happy.

It had not been easy at all, but it would have been if she had known he was going to call.

He said he had tried to bury himself in the study of cave paintings in modern-day France, a subject that had interested him for some time, but he had not been able to concentrate at all.

'I can't concentrate either,' she said. 'Haven't got a thing done today.'

He gave a doubtful laugh, said he was tired and that perhaps they ought to sleep tonight, not having done much sleeping the previous night, that is, sleep apart.

'Perhaps that would be best,' she said.

This put her in a quandary. She could not decide whether he had said they should sleep apart in order for her to contradict him, or because he actually wanted to. In short, she didn't know if she should insist or if that would seem nagging and clingy. She remained passive to be on the safe side, so as not to be a bother or to let her reproachfulness show.

———

He was working day, evening and night on his next piece of video art. But when they spoke on Sunday they had agreed, or had some sort of implicit understanding, that they would meet on Tuesday. They had not set a time, however. He perceived time differently from her. She was accustomed to exact times and mutually agreed meetings, appointments that one kept.

From five o'clock on Tuesday she sat at home, waiting for a signal that he was ready. She thought they would start by going out to dinner and then go up to his place, sit on the sofa and then go to bed.

She waited, not knowing what time he had anticipated they would meet, or even whether they definitely would.

He was working. He was always hard at it, working.

He rang at around midnight. He was finished. And ready. She had cleaned her teeth, had a shower, put on clean clothes and had time to swear, and curse him loudly to herself. Now, she dashed straight out and ran full pelt to the bus stop, the taste of iron in her mouth. She ran from his stop at Karlavägen, too, tapped in the door code he had given her and took the steps two at a time. He received her with a wine glass in his hand and a beaming face, stroked her arm up and down, and gently took her hand.

'May I show you what I've been up to?'

She looked carefully at everything he showed her in the studio.

'I don't understand how one can have this sort of talent,' she said, 'how one learns to do it.'

'It's nice to hear you say that,' he said. 'You're usually so critical.'

'Critical, me? I'm no expert on this sort of thing and I view it with love because it's you who made it.'

'Ah. Yes.'

He seemed embarrassed but at the same time, and primarily, proud of his domain and its theatrical set pieces.

'Love is not cool and scrutinizing,' said Ester. 'Surely you must see the difference?'

He took her hand in his again, pointing with the other one.

'It's called *trompe-l'œil*,' he said, looking at her to observe how the term went down and whether it would be insulting to translate it or inconsiderate not to.

'You know about *trompe-l'œil*?'

'Never seen it but I've heard about it. Striking effect.'

'It means "deceive the eye".'

It involved painting the sets with distorted proportions and in small sizes so that what was represented would appear in realistic perspective in the picture. Great cities or expanses of landscape could spring from something the size of a matchbox.

They embraced beneath his sets. He explained that these were intended to deceive the eye with regard to distance, size and ultimately the whole of existence. They were poetic truths, built to make the eye see the world as it was although everything was false, or stage-managed.

They went across the courtyard and upstairs to his flat.

The banks of snow were dirty white and shone dimly in the gleam of the pale lights.

He entered without a key, telling her he always left the door unlocked because there was nothing to steal. Then he took off his work clothes and had a shower while she looked round. It was the first time she had been in his home. It was scarcely a home, more like sleeping quarters. Everything was provisional, including the rack where he hung shirts and jackets, which stood near his bed. Wardrobes were evidently not for him.

It was as if he were travelling, or on the run. From what he had said and what she now saw, Ester sensed more about his mentality. She realized he thought of the future as a state completely removed from the present. The future was something that would follow great change and bring rest. One day, real life would begin, once he had finished all this work. Soon he would have time to get to grips with everything, once that solo exhibition was out of the way and that retrospective. That was his ideology, and his view of society too; deep down, he was a revolutionary utopian. Paradise was not merely a word.

It was one way to spend a life. You could get a lot done while you waited for life to begin.

When Hugo came out of the bathroom, Ester was already lying under the cover.

'That looks cosy,' he said, abandoning his towel on a chair by the bed and lying down by her, skin against skin.

'This is the supreme moment,' she whispered. 'The supreme moment in human life. This encounter. The greatest thing there is.'

He answered her with his hands.

On waking the next morning they fumbled for each other and started all over again. Their coupling was briefer but as ardent as before. It was eight o'clock and the working day was waiting. He observed that he had nothing to eat in the flat, a possible indication that his earlier comment about breakfast as mere nutritional refuelling did have some kind of validity for him and had not just been an excuse to avoid intimacy. She hoped as much, and felt everything pointed to it. She wondered whether she should suggest right now that they see each other again that evening and not leave things to run their course so it was all just more waiting and she could not make other plans.

But she could not quite bring herself to.

He asked her to come with him down to the 7-Eleven store on the corner. There he had coffee and a croissant while she had coffee and a bread roll, solid rye with no filling. It was one of the more rudimentary breakfasts in her life.

They perched beside each other on tall stools at a shelf-like table under the window, looking out over an intersection and the morning activity of a city street. They said little. When they did speak, it was about generalities, things they could see, how the coffee tasted and what was on the menu. They were neither friends nor lovers. They asked each other what they had planned for the day, in the way you do when you don't belong together even though you are sleeping with each other, that is, when one party has decided how things are to be on that score but not said so openly, believing it is meant to be inferred.

Ester had no wish to tell him what she would be doing that day. She did not know what she would be doing and the question was of so little interest. She wanted him to ask: What shall we do today? What would you like us to do today? Not the rejection of: What are you doing today?

Hugo talked about the weather and the temperature, the fact that it was perishing cold and a hard winter, and that many found the cold difficult. She said:

'It's exactly halfway through the winter.'

Then she thought she ought to say that she liked the winter, but there was no space for such a remark. What she liked did not feel relevant; they were not engaged in getting to know each other, after all.

A complete lack of contact prevailed between them, a ghastly alienation. He was sitting beside her in a public place and thus not disowning her. He was eating breakfast with her the morning after, albeit a basic one. It should have been a matter of simply falling into it. But they were strangers to each other. This encounter was its own outward incarnation. It had no real content and was therefore bursting with other, unspoken content.

'What happens if your colleagues see us together?' she asked.

He appeared not to understand the question.

'I mean if they see us like this in the morning, now, at eight o'clock.'

'But we don't talk about that sort of thing.'

She found his answer peculiar, somehow illogical. The important thing, surely, was what the others knew and how significant that was for him? Whether they talked about it or not ought to be a secondary issue. She considered starting a discussion of his answer, analysing it thoroughly and thus finding another way of letting all the disappointment she felt come bubbling out. He downed the rest of his coffee and dismounted from his stool.

'I've got to go.'

She nodded. He was experiencing a diffuse sense of guilt. It was detectable in a certain slight lag in the way he moved his head; it disturbed his brow, the corners of his eyes and his posture.

'Are you going to stay here a bit longer and philosophize?' he said.

'Yes. I'll philosophize for a while.'

He leant forward and kissed her cheek. A distinct, affectionate, loving kiss. It was also a kiss that knew something about inadequacy. He stood still, hesitating, before he left.

She stayed a bit longer but did not philosophize. It was a Wednesday with a whitish haze of the sort that found its way under your collar. A day full of forebodings. Something was seriously wrong, she knew. Not with their encounter so much as in their different views of its gravity and significance.

Nothing had been said about how things would carry on and nothing about their entry into each other's lives or the muteness that had followed it. Nothing about anything.

They had stopped talking the moment their bodies took over. Love needs no words. For a short period you can put your trust in wordless emotion. But in the long run there is no love without words, and no love with words alone. Love is a hungry beast. It lives off touch, repeated assurances and an eye that looks deeply into another eye. When that eye is right up close to the other eye, neither of them sees a thing.

She sat there for a quarter of an hour and then took the bus home. The air did not lighten all day and he did not call. Nor did she, but when she did not call it meant something different from him not calling, because he decided, he had the power. There was no evidence and yet no doubt that this was the case. The one applying the brake is always the one who decides. The one who wants least has the most power. When he did not call, it was hardly because he thought: I'd better restrain myself and not keep calling.

This is hell, she thought the next morning when twenty-four hours had passed. This is what hell feels like and this is a hell that actually exists. She was burning up from inside.

On Thursday evening Ester was due to attend a party to which Hugo had also been invited. They had spoken of this a couple of weeks earlier but then it had gone out of her mind, when they hit upon more pleasant reasons for assignations.

By then she had recovered from the hellish visions of that morning and a certain sense of anticipation crept in. It was a chance to meet, after all. Admittedly she could not ignore the significance of his failure to call or the fact that they were not in contact, even though this was precisely the period when contact should have been at its most frenzied. She knew it was not mere chance that nothing was happening; it corresponded to some psychological phenomenon for which there was presumably a precise term. But she tried to convince herself that it was mere chance, that things sometimes just happened, that people were different, that some were in frequent touch and others less so, regardless of how much they felt, and that beginnings were always tricky and tentative.

She didn't believe her own mantra. She was just trying to appease the fates. She was convinced that what was happening could be traced back to realities. His non-action in not ringing her, even though he ought to want to, corresponded to a movement in his brain, a movement that was the result of a deliberation, albeit only at the level of perception, and of an absence of movement in his heart. She had sensed clearly and intensely that this deliberation was doing nothing to promote the progress of their love, their future relationship.

But he was also a hard-working man, she thought. She ought not to anticipate unhappiness that might never materialize. She should be bright and cheerful when they met that evening, not reveal anything of the thoughts and emotions raging within her.

By now it was afternoon. In the course of the day she had called him six times. He doubtless had a lot to do and was not near his phone. She thought it was a shame that he did not long for her enough to want to call even though he hadn't time, that he did not keep the phone with him so as not to miss a single call from her as she would have done, behaviour that would normally characterize the stage they had now reached. Had she reached it alone? Or did his longing express itself in other ways?

It was the sort of day when she could not keep thought and feeling apart.

Heavy of heart, she went to the party. Once she was there she managed to shake off some of her uneasiness, chatted to people, laughed, ate and drank. At ten o'clock he had still not arrived. At eleven, a good number of people started to leave. Then he came, in a taxi. He had a smallish entourage with him, associates from the studio who had not been invited, among them Dragan. Since starting to keep company with Hugo, Ester had learned that Dragan was of Yugoslavian birth and had come to Sweden in 1981, with predilections for French philosophy and a sophisticated variant of Communism. Dragan had supported the mullahs in Iran in 1979 to defy Western hegemony and saw no reason to comment on or revise his standpoint thereafter. Most things were abstractions to him and as an abstraction this stance functioned well, in his view. Ester asked him how he could live with the consequences but he had dismissed her as an imperialist lackey and mental colonizer. Hugo Rask admired his friend and shared his contempt for all that smacked of liberalism, the West and bourgeois respectability, anything *comme il faut*. Socialists they might be, Ester told them sometimes, but they perpetually ended up in the laps of the conservatives, sometimes even dangerously close to a fascist world view. At that, Dragan would give a snort and call her a conformist and careerist, two labels he was always very ready to distribute, and declared that she had better go home and read up on it, because at this level it was beneath him to refute her assertions. Dragan had private financial means and did not need to work, it was said, though nobody knew the details, but ever since his arrival in Sweden he had acted as an informal adviser and companion to Hugo Rask. He spoke Swedish with a strong accent and excellent grammar. For decades the two confrères had sat in Hugo's premises talking of the rotten state of the world and what to do about it. They had even done a number of things to excise the rot, everyone had to admit. Ester had devoured it all with famished energy: books, films, brochures and documentary accounts of past happenings that she had unearthed from the archive.

To start with, as Dragan sat there in the studio in the evenings smoking his eternal cigarettes, he had looked condescendingly and disdainfully at Ester, as if he knew something he was not revealing. Ester wanted to ask him what it was he knew, but realized where his loyalty lay.

Hugo had never distanced himself from any of the malice to which Dragan's refined thinking inadvertently led. He had too much of a taste for provocation as a life-style to repudiate violence and oppression in the name of revolt.

What was strange about Hugo Rask, thought Ester Nilsson, was that the only thing to attract him more than provocation was being loved by the public. It was pulling him apart, because at the same time he could not bear being loved by the public, believing it to signal complicity, cowardice and indifference in the face of the raw truths which no present day had ever had the courage to confront but which the future always saw uncomfortably clearly, with an indulgent smile at the narrow outlook of times past.

With defiant pride, Dragan and Hugo had lined up behind Milošević in Serbia. This was still viewed as an embarrassing blot on the artist's public image, something that had to be touched on in any tribute article so the writer could not be accused of playing down the artist's poor judgement and unforgivable lapse, or perhaps it was the complexity of his soul. It was a stance that had come at some cost, including several cancelled exhibitions. Ester once asked him about it, and received the answer that he was not interested in anything that was held in wide affection, was uniform or imposed by the elite. She was not offered any arguments in support of his position. She wanted to ask more, wanted to hear how he reconciled such slogans with being so desperately anxious personally for the public's affection.

But she had swallowed her questions in order not to jeopardize their fragile intimacy.

Dragan made his entry to the party in a black suit, black polo-necked sweater and the elegant black shoes he had been wearing the first time she met him. He gave a malicious wave in her direction.

'So you're here too?' he said.

The fact that Hugo was surrounded by his own people even here at the party considerably reduced her opportunities for wondering out loud about all those unanswered phone calls and other things that had failed to happen. His face shone like a round red cheese when he saw her, a nervous, uncomfortable, round red cheese. From that point he was always half turned away, making off somewhere, as if in fear of questions. When he finally met her eye he did it with an insouciance that was almost brazen.

'Have you missed me?'

The question was entirely rhetorical, a laboured game.

'Yes. I have. A lot.'

Her words thudded clumsily to the floor between them and died. She did not return the question, to avoid hearing the answer and seeing him discomfited by the need for evasion.

'Shall we try the buffet?' he said.

'I already have,' she said. 'It's delicious.'

'Oh, um,' he said, apparently disconcerted by the fact that she had thought he was addressing her. He indicated with a nod and a gesture that the invitation was meant not for her but for the friends he had brought with him, famished after their day's strenuous labour among set pieces and constructions designed to deceive the eye.

His spite was not deliberate or studied. It was simple omission, inability, fear disguised as considerate behaviour. Ester left them to it and went to talk to other people, kept her distance.

As the party began to feel past its prime, she sought him out again. She had weighed it up and reached the decision that she would rather be brushed off than fret about not having tried. He was discussing something with a journalist, one of the arts editors. Dragan was standing with them. All three were laughing, in relaxed agreement over something. Ester put her hand on Hugo's back. He looked at her with eyes that were swivelling round in their sockets in search of an emergency exit. Somewhere inside herself she understood that this was answer enough, but she could not bear it. She took him to one side and asked:

'Shall we go back to my place?'

She steeled herself not to offer him freedom at the same time. If he wanted to run away he would have to organize it himself.

'If we're going, it had better be my place,' he said.

She wanted to say they should forget all about it, but stayed silent.

They went out into the street. The streetlights gleamed coldly in the black-white night. They walked three blocks to a more major road, where a taxi soon came along. It struck her that this was exactly where she had been when, bathed in spring sunshine, she took the call asking her to give a lecture on him. Now it was night and winter in the same spot. He held the back door of the car open for her and they got in. She took his hand to give it a squeeze but the hand squirmed like a captured maggot, trying to extract itself from hers without making it too obvious.

Unsolicited gifts can be appalling in their demands, their expectations, their sticky demonstration of the giver's solicitude. It was not impossible that he looked on her pressurizing hand as such a gift. He tried to stroke her fingers but it was more like rubbing. He seemed in the grip of some great torment that transmitted itself through his hand.

She did not understand what that torment could be. She did not think she was demanding anything unreasonable. Freedom was a virtue and she honoured it, but she could not offer freedom from closeness. What she could offer, on the other hand, was the freedom to be closer to her than anyone else, and the freedom to escape his loneliness. What could be more beautiful?

The taxi stopped at the front entrance of his building. He let go of her fingers, took out his wallet, paid. Had it been up to her they would have taken the bus, so she let him pay.

The third night. Three nights in five days can't be put down to mistake, whim or aberration. They climbed the stairs to his inhospitable little den for this, their third night. They undressed, their bodies joined. They went to sleep. Morning came again. Their bodies joined again. But something was wrong. Something was wrong the whole time.

He kept his blinds closed round the clock; except for a broken slat where the light shone in you could not tell whether it was night or day, clear or overcast.

The light coming through the gap showed that it was now morning. He touched her in the right ways. He knew how you show that you want to be present, but he was absent, and tense and evasive with it, afraid that by talking they would find a vein from which difficulties would come gushing forth.

He was soon dressed and ready to go, before she was, even though they were in his flat. It looked as though he wanted to get out so he could breathe, as if he were escaping to an oxygen cylinder.

'There's bread and cheese,' he said.

'Aren't you going to have anything?'

'I've got to get down to the studio and work. I think there's coffee as well. I did some shopping.'

'Who for?'

'You said breakfast was important to you.'

She kissed his closed lips and he went. So he had been out to buy breakfast for her after Wednesday morning's foray to 7-Eleven, that is, he had planned to bring her here again. In that case, why was he behaving so strangely?

The sense of desolation in a flat that your lover has just left is the most complete sense of desolation that exists. It hit her now.

It's not worth it, she felt.

It's always worth it, she thought.

Worth it or not, I can't give it up, she thought and felt.

She sat down to eat in his untouched kitchen. Piles of newspapers were stacked along the lower parts of the walls, several years' worth of the *Dagens Nyheter* and *Svenska Dagbladet* review sections. He was doubtless saving them because there was an essay or opinion piece he had not managed to read at the time but imagined he would get round to later.

In that respect he's an optimist in the midst of all his pessimism, she thought. Optimist in the same sense as utopians are, and Marxist-inspired pessimists. One day he would find the strength to do what was beyond him now. He put things off and dreamt of the state in which everything would be different. She did not, and she seldom put things off. Paradise was a logical nullity because life was friction and friction could only disappear at death. Life was composed merely of an endless series of small nows in which one lacked the energy to do what one wanted to do. There was no later, because later, too, would prove to be a now that was also deficient in energy. She believed in the paradise of two people meeting. Having experienced it, she knew it not to be a utopia. As an anti-utopian she did not believe she would find the energy to read articles she could not be bothered with now, and whatever society and individual human beings were incapable of now, they would remain incapable of later.

She looked at his piles of newspapers, so full of hope, and felt jealous of them. He hoarded yellowing old newspapers but he let her go to waste. The world was more important. She felt downcast, sitting there in his white, dead kitchen, and lines from Sonja Åkesson's poem *Autobiography* came into her mind:

'I seek a healthy soul in a healthy body. I have saved at

least a hundred copies of *Dagens Nyheter* and really do intend to follow the debate one day. I see another war unroll across the black-and-white pages. I ran out into the early dusk and wanted to put my hand through the sky, but hurried back home so as not to burn the potatoes.'

She ate some of the bread and cheese he had bought for her, at least perhaps it was for her he had bought it, and drank a large cup of black coffee that she brewed in his coffee maker. That, too, appeared unused.

She thought of his weaknesses as an artist. The work he created was received as great visual poetry, but while some of it was interesting and original, it suffered from the same shortcomings as its creator. He dared not enter into his own pain and hence not into the pain of others, either. He did not know what pain was. He observed it from outside but did not feel it, and therefore did not reach as deeply in his portrayals of human beings as his thirst for greatness demanded. Those involuntary lies and that teetering on the edge of humanity kept him from what he was seeking. Whenever it started to get painful, he turned away, both in his self-absorption and in his observation of the world around him. From fear of what he might find, he dared not seek inside himself to understand what was in other people. He did not want to understand what was in other people, for they might harbour aggressions and reproaches directed at him. Thus he preferred not to face existence and see it for what it was, for all he claimed to do so. He observed people from outside, in a behaviourist light, never a phenomenological one. He wanted to accuse, not understand. This led to art with limitations. But no one was as good at making a virtue of their limitations as he was, hiding the weaknesses and making it look virtuosic. That was his great talent, the one with which he deceived the world. That was where his artistic strength lay.

With a vindictiveness that took her by surprise, her opinions of his insignificance came tumbling out. She came to the view that it was magnanimous of her to love him in spite of these deficiencies and that he ought to be grateful.

When she had finished eating and washed up, she put a note in the fridge with one of the commonest declarations of love that language has to offer. Subject, predicate, object.

The note had an unmistakable element of persuasion about it. It was an appeal and a shackle. As she closed the fridge door she saw a box of natural cold remedy lying on the worktop, and another handwritten note: 'Take these and you'll soon feel better!!! Love, Eva-Stina'.

The three exclamation marks indicated either a poor sense of style or an overwhelming urge to be heard. She remembered he had had a cold just after the Christmas holidays. They had met and gone out for a meal even though he was coughing and snuffling.

Eva-Stina was the young woman who worked for him, the one who had given her a sideways look the previous autumn. You didn't write a note like that unless you really liked someone, you just wouldn't phrase it that way. A note was always significant, not primarily for what it said, but for the act, the writing of the note. And that applied equally to the note she had just left on the top shelf of the refrigerator, even if that was more explicit. It did not only say, 'I love you.' If you factored in the circumstances, the background, her personality, the context and subtext, it said something more like: 'I love you with all my soul, I'm nice to you all the time, I want only good things for us, so why do you assert the right to behave the way you do?'

Putting together the natural remedy and the thoughtful line of writing, the sideways looks that Eva-Stina had given her and the memory of Hugo a few weeks ago, uncharacteristically scratching his head and saying, 'That girl with the double name I can never remember,' Ester divined that this was not innocent. This note was more than a note. Eva-Stina lurked there in the offing, biding her time, with constant access to him because they worked together. Or were they already in a relationship? Was that why he had been so odd over the past few days?

It was impossible. In that case he wouldn't have wanted her round at his place last night or the night before and he ought not to have suggested breakfast down on the corner on Wednesday.

She collected her things and herself, and left his flat.

She brooded as she walked to the bus stop. After all, some people were prepared to organize their love lives that way, or rather their sex lives, having several partners simultaneously without letting on. Strangely enough they were the same people who were surprised and irritated by how much bother it was to juggle times, lies, assignations and other people's actual, existing existences, and all that these involved in terms of demands, expectations and yearning. Necrophilia would be the best thing for people like that, she thought. The undemanding dead would be ideal for terribly busy, hardworking, highly sexed geniuses.

All that day she carried on thinking about his weaknesses as an artist. It eased the hurt a little.

Ever since he had suggested dinner at Ester's so that a union of their flesh could occur, she had assumed that in doing so he had ended the supposed relationship with the supposed woman in the south of Sweden. Everything pointed to her having been more of a convenience than a love affair. Although travelling that far every other weekend was naturally a token of something. It was hardly something you undertook for the sake of convenience.

Ester thought it had taken him so long to come to her because he wanted to resolve everything first; that he had waited so things would all be lovely between them. Pure and lovely.

The day, which was a Friday, passed slowly. Anxiety weighed like a painful, nagging stone inside her. She told herself that people who have entered into the union of bodies and love each other have to have trust. There was a lot speaking in their favour. Now she just needed steel in her belly rather than this stone.

Since their relationship had become sexual they had not discussed essential topics even once, but there would be time for that, too. Anything important took time. There was a time for everything. Everything was fine. It had all gone better than she could have dreamt of, that Saturday in October, and the outcome she had craved so madly in November and December had materialized. She had everything she had fantasized about. It was unbelievable. Everything looked bright. It was a day filled with light. And yet another day on which she was incapable of writing. What little she did get down came out as dead phrases, spreading the smell of corpses across the text.

Friday limped on. The most common question since the invention of the telephone could very well be: Why doesn't he ring? She lay down on the bed and read Mayakovsky's poem 'A Cloud in Trousers', because he had claimed it was important. The title was fantastic; the poem had its good points but much of it left her unmoved. She was by turns furious with him and filled with enormous tenderness and love for everything he had ever touched or been touched by (with certain obvious exceptions).

She had made up her mind not to ring him. He was

hard at work; she must show him respect and demonstrate that she was a self-sufficient, independent, autonomous grown-up perfectly able to cope without constant contact. Admittedly she thought it was strange that one would not want perpetual contact with the person with whom one had just embarked on a loving relationship, but she had to be flexible.

She changed books and read some of *Hitler's Table Talk*, which he had also recommended. He had wanted to study the book in order to comprehend how things could go the way they did and to learn to recognize the signs in time. Everywhere in the contemporary world he saw signs that Nazism and fascism were continually latent in those societies ruled by parliamentary pseudo-democracy. He saw this particularly clearly when he had been talking to Dragan a lot.

Ester read. She was absolutely not going to call him today. She called. He didn't answer. Eight o'clock came. She wondered what could explain his not wanting to be with her on their first Friday evening together. She didn't understand. But one can't push things. One must never push things. Just be considerate and accommodating yet avoid becoming stifling. There are natural explanations for everything, she thought. He was in a concentrated working phase. He felt secure with her and did not need to keep telling her what he was doing, or making contact, because they were in continuous spiritual contact anyway. They knew where they were with each other.

What she must definitely not do now was to expose herself to the anguish of sending a text message that would go unanswered. The anguish generated by the non-appearance of an answer was something the creators of texts and emails could not have anticipated. Or perhaps they lacked that kind of empathy? Your fingers burned after you had texted and experienced the relief inherent in sending something off, which persisted for some minutes afterwards, while some hope of an answer still remained. She picked up her mobile more than once and began tapping in a message, but deleted it every time and put the phone down.

When she woke up it was Saturday. She could not work that day either. For her, writing was never escape, it was resistance, and resistance is nothing to escape to. She had to occupy herself with something while waiting for her life to start. She looked at the phone. Perhaps she had it on silent by mistake? No. No one had called, and no text message had arrived unnoticed. She rang herself from her landline to check her mobile was working. Sent herself a text. Everything worked as it should.

She ventured out into the city. It was cold outside. It was around midday, in fact getting on for one. She wandered about, had a Turkish burger in the indoor food market in Hötorgshallen and strolled aimlessly through a few clothes shops, feeling the fabrics between finger and thumb. If he would only get in touch and tell her what was going on, that was all she wanted. He had bought breakfast for her some time between Wednesday morning and Thursday evening. That must mean that he etc. She went down Kungsgatan, across Stureplan and on down Birger Jarlsgatan. In Rönnells' second-hand bookshop she saw a book she wanted to give him, but decided to postpone all such purchases until the following week. She did not know whether he wanted any more books from her or whether they would even be seeing each other again. She didn't understand. The worst part of all was not understanding this thing she was in the midst of, this thing that had her in its clutches. There is no pain like the pain of not understanding.

It was three o'clock and he had not called. She had coffee in a cafe and an extra-large pastry with it, on account of the situation. There was a book in front of her that she was trying to read. It was four o'clock. She went to the cinema to see a film about the CIA, one of those films she never really managed to keep up with but could not work out what she was missing either. As the film was showing she thought how relieved she would be if he rang at that precise moment. All the knots in her body would suddenly loosen as if they had never existed and she would become human again. Not even he could work non-stop. But perhaps this really was an extremely intensive phase.

She did not understand this CIA film, either. The plots were made for the people who wrote them and not for the audience, she thought. They had spent so long writing their scripts that all the events seemed self-evident to them. They wrote the work backwards whereas the viewers saw it forwards.

Something came into her mind, which she then formulated in the minutes that followed.

The physicists' problem:

That we don't remember things that have not yet happened.

The philosophers' problem:

That we remember something merely because it has happened.

The psychologists' problem:

That we remember what suits us.

The politicians' problem:

That people have a memory.

The medics' problem:

That memory fails us.

The unhappy lovers' problem:

That the memory of what has happened alters us.

She looked around the auditorium. The audience was sparse but those who were there looked attentive. Perhaps they were the sort who did not spend their time suffering and being tormented, the sort who had a life both now and when the film was over.

All at once she had a very definite premonition and could see in her mind's eye that she and Hugo would meet that evening, eat, drink, laugh, make love. He would ring her any moment now, bellow cheerily and this nightmare would be over.

'What are you doing this evening? Are you hungry?' he would shout, and she would not reveal with a single sound how she had been feeling – never reproach – but simply say:

'Yes! I'm hungry! What time?'

Within an hour or so they would be sitting in a restaurant and with sparkling eyes he would reach out his
hand and touch her cheek. She had been in agonies before,
believing it was all over, just before he got in touch. The
important thing was to hold on, not hang up.

The realization crashed in on her like a meteorite and its
impact was as violent as the one seventy million years
earlier that wiped out the dinosaurs. She no longer saw
what was happening on the cinema screen in front of her
as everything in her body went into reverse in a single diz-
zying second and the true state of affairs dawned on her. It
was obvious yet inconceivable: naturally he was with his
woman in Malmö this weekend. The last time had been a
fortnight ago and he was there every other weekend, always
had been. Atomic clocks could be set by his trips to Malmö.
The previous Saturday they had met at Ester's house and
this weekend it was Malmö's turn again. The thought had
not occurred to her even once during the preceding week
because the act was too preposterous, but it explained his
behaviour in recent days.

The film was only halfway through. She sat on while the
blackest anguish she had ever felt rolled through her in
wave after wave of arsenic and lead.

Why was she staying? Because there was nothing else to
do and nowhere else to go anyway, in that moment at

which her suspicions had been confirmed. She might just as well sit in a cinema.

After the film she walked up to his street. The weather was raw and drearily grey, no temptation to evening strollers. The street lights were on, the shopkeepers were switching off the lights in their back rooms, locking up with jangling bunches of keys and sighing with relief at the prospect of their free Sundays. Ester headed towards his block to find out for sure.

The reason it had taken her so long to realize was that she could not understand how a person who did that sort of thing looked on life and on other people. Her whole idea of humanity as one, and psychically homogenous, had been rocked to its foundations. This way of dealing with the material world was too strange.

Even from a distance she could see that the studio was bolted and barred. Clearly she had still been nourishing a glimmer of hope in spite of everything, because the certainty inflicted more pain. It was only when he was away that the studio was shut up and the wrought-iron outer gate was locked. There were no sets being built here this evening. She went across the yard and up to his flat and peered in through the letterbox. No light anywhere.

Hugo had given her to understand there were people at work in the studio from morning to night and every day, weekends too. He had let her believe he was a busy man, a relentlessly working artist who was not to be disturbed and on whom no one could place any demands because he was working for art, which was all about how human beings behave towards one another, about casual evil, the exercise of power and powerlessness. But just now he was taking a rest from that.

There were patches of ice on the ground and the wind crept stealthily along the streets, whipped round corners and jabbed its malevolent needles into necks and wrists. The temperature hovered between melting and refreezing. Slush by day, a thin crust of ice by evening.

Once again she walked from his studio to the bus. As she took her seat she got out her phone and started composing a text message. She had finished it by the time she got off the bus a quarter of an hour later and she sent it off with no thought of refraining. It was a highly condensed communication, as strained as dread and panic become when they conceal themselves behind haughtiness. Its tone exuded contempt rooted in self-respect. It was a message you could cut yourself on. And she censured him with all the justification of the scorned.

But it was text, it was not her, it was her as text. In the physical world there was neither haughtiness nor self-respect. In this physical world, she was on the point of collapsing into a loose heap.

A brief triumph presented itself, however, once the message was sent. Both the act of writing it and the opportunity of directing her anger at him in hard, well-formulated thrusts eased the pain for a while. And it was contact, some form of human encounter that broke the unbearable silence. He would read the message and think of her, and answer.

But no answer came. Nothing came at all. Saturday evening went by. Sunday went by. On the Monday morning, thirty-six hours had passed without a word from Hugo. It was a perfect demonstration of how to kill a person by social means.

She went down to the Central Station in the middle of the day and positioned herself where the Malmö trains came in, but it was futile. There were hourly arrivals and her chances of striking lucky were slim. Crowds of people came streaming off the many carriages of the train towards a host of underpasses, exits and stairways, and she did not see him. She stood there waiting for two hours, three arrivals. Then she went back home and wrote an email in which she drily analysed the whole sequence of events.

'The more you stay silent the more I speak, it's Hegelian,' she wrote, and was embarrassed by her own pretensions but left them in anyway. She put forward all the objective eventualities she could think of to account for his acting as he had, and set out all the conceivable and self-critical points of view, future prospects and inter-pretations that her imagination could muster, except one: that she had no right to an explanation. She drew the line there. She wrote that she understood that you couldn't speak the truth if you lived in a world where you would be punished for it, and that her moral rules were perhaps too strict for him to want to speak the truth. She suggested that she had gone too fast and not listened to his needs or tempo. But she considered she had the right to an explanation because they had a contract with one another. He had assumed responsibility by entering her body; that amounted to holding out to her the prospect that something had to be carried through. Hence she had rights, and they included hearing his explanation.

She left no perspective unexplored except the one that said she had no rights. It did not occur to her to have such a dispassionate relationship with life or to have such contempt for herself. Elements in the girlfriend chorus found it hard to put up with this lack of acceptance, or, as Ester saw it, this lack of self-contempt. They, having put so much effort into eradicating their needs in order to please, or behaving properly and not disturbing anyone, were irritated by Ester's self-righteousness in not realizing that she was not wanted. He owes you nothing, they told her. She examined their argument and found that she did not share their analysis.

Strength and competence arouse admiration, but not love. It's the shortcomings in a person that inspire love. But those shortcomings are not enough. They have to be complemented by autonomy and self-distance. Flaws create affection, but sooner or later aggressions will be generated by the very thing that arouses affection. Pure deficiency is in its helplessness as impossible to love as steely strength.

Ester got no answer, regardless of whether she felt strong, weak or ridden with flaws. The whole week passed with no sign of life from him.

Her breathing was shallow and she felt permanently tight across the chest. Every evening she took the bus to his street. Lights shone from the windows once more and work was in progress in the studio. The person she had gone to sleep and woken up with, and two weeks ago had laughed with and talked to for hours, was now someone she had to stand and look at from a street corner, like before it all started.

On the Friday, a week after the last time they had seen each other, that last morning a thousand years ago, she made a decision and once more took the bus to his place.

Enough was enough; she was not prepared to accept any more of this cowardly evasion.

It was six in the evening. She entered the studio without ringing the bell, and went upstairs. There on the first floor, behind the big, solid desk, she found him working. He looked over his glasses, neither dismayed nor afraid nor glad. He said:

'You're here.'

'Yes. I am.'

He rested his elbows on the table, held his hands loosely clasped, and did not reveal what he was thinking. Ester asked if they could talk, said it was vital, and though he showed no great enthusiasm they crossed the road to the local restaurant where they used to sit by candlelight. It was now an unfamiliar place in her eyes. But the staff greeted them warmly as two regulars and immediately prepared their favourite table in the corner.

She heard him tell the waitress that they wouldn't be staying very long.

Still on his feet, he ordered a glass of wine for himself. The waitress waited attentively but discreetly for another order. And when it did not come she moved towards the kitchen. At the same moment Hugo gave Ester a quick glance and said perhaps she wanted something as well? She nodded.

Hugo sat on the edge of the chair with most of his body weight on his lower legs and feet, he twisted and shuffled and looked at anything but her, poised for a hasty exit.

She saw it, but what she felt was love. There was no longer any need for explanations. Everything she had wanted to ask, all those breathless ideas, turned out to have been an excuse to spend time in his company. She wanted them to keep seeing each other, that was the long and the short of it. She wanted to have a relationship, that was all. She missed him enormously, it was as simple as that. She wanted them to sit together, talking for hours, and then go on home to his place and wake up in the morning with a long Saturday stretching before them. When they were together she lacked for nothing.

'I'll have to get back soon,' he said, his flickering gaze bouncing briefly into her own. 'Lots to do. A terrifically intense phase of work.'

The illusion shattered and the coolness returned. The meeting she had obtained by force had to be justified and explained anew with harsh imperatives like morality and the need to understand, not with the softness of her thoughts a moment before.

She had a good mind to say he had been in a terrifically intense phase of work the previous weekend, too, but decided not to be sarcastic. One always came to regret sarcasms.

'I did all I could to make contact,' she said.

'I noticed.'

There was silence while she absorbed this snide remark.

'Why didn't you answer?'

'What bit was I meant to answer, given everything you

were asking? You were wondering about so much. In fact I don't think I've ever seen so many questions all in one place.'

'I texted you as well. And phoned.'

'Yes. You did.'

'Do you mean the email I sent on Monday?'

'I don't know what day it came. It wasn't feasible to answer all those questions.'

'Do you think there might be a reason why I've had so much to wonder about this past week?'

'No idea.'

'No. Sometimes it's difficult to see how things are connected.'

He emptied his glass in a couple of hurried gulps.

Her breath came in little gasps.

'The reason I had so many questions was that your behaviour's been incomprehensible. For three months we've been seeing each other and developing some kind of intimacy. It culminates in three erotic encounters that I assume we both considered inevitable. Three erotic encounters in the space of six nights. Since then your behaviour has been obnoxious, and what's more, obnoxious in a singularly mysterious way. So I'm left guessing. Anybody wanting to torture a person only has to do what you've been doing to me this past week.'

He said nothing. Twirled his empty glass, scanned the restaurant. He didn't look as though he felt any sense of guilt and he didn't appear to be keeping quiet because he was unsure what to say. All he wanted was to get out of the shackles she had put on him and he was keeping quiet in the way one does with somebody who isn't going to understand in any case, who inhabits another world with different rules of play, pointless to discuss because of the gaping chasm in between.

'I've been desperate all week. I don't know what to do.'

'If you're down you ought to go and talk to someone.'

'I am talking to someone. Right now.'

'Someone who knows about these things. A professional.'

'Who knows about broken hearts? There's one person who can help me with my problem, and that's you.'

'I'm afraid I've got to get back to work now.'

From the dull tone of his voice and the tired look in his eye she could detect that awareness of inadequacy again. An inadequacy that had ossified into an abstract loathing of women for their eternal amorous demands on a person like him, with bigger things to think about, their prattle and possessive impositions tossed out like lassoes, always excused in their view by their tenderly throbbing hearts.

'It was passion,' he said. 'It seized us, as passions do. Perhaps you in particular.'

'Thanks, it's remarkably kind of you to say so.'

'But true. You were clearly more affected than I was. I haven't been feeling desperate.'

The ill will or hatred behind his words made everything swim, as if the oxygen were running out.

'So passion isn't love, in your world?'

'They're different things.'

'Not even related?'

'Distantly perhaps. But one doesn't go on long summer holidays with an object of one's passion or live with them for years.'

'What an interesting definition. But it doesn't seem universally applicable, which presumably makes it worthless as a definition. I'd be very happy to go on long summer holidays with you and to live with you for the rest of eternity. Winter holidays, too.'

'But I wouldn't.'

'So it's been nothing to do with love, what we've had? I'm so glad you've solved that one.'

He ran his teeth over his lips, a little dry and flaky from the cold weather, though the crack had healed. His body was tense but he let his shoulders droop with a sigh.

'You got so bloody angry on Saturday. That text you sent was pretty scary. Enough to make anyone back off. Things could get too unpleasant.'

'And you really can't understand why I was angry?'

'Well, maybe I can.'

'You don't think, after all there's been between us, all we've done together and everything it implied, that I've got a right to be upset, that I've got a right to know what you think about you and me? You've laid claim to me. You've been inside my body. Don't you think that puts me in some sort of privileged position in which your integrity has to yield and it's kind of incumbent on you to talk to me about actions you take that affect me so badly I can actually hardly stand upright? The anguish of this is killing me.'

'But you've already got the answers. These aren't questions. They're assertions and accusations. Everything's already clear, in your exemplary judgement. All you've got to do is force me into confession and submission and then you're done.'

'I detest submission. The only thing I want is for us to be together, and close to each other mentally. That's all I wish for. Why didn't you try to meet me halfway instead of going mute and silent? We'd established a relationship. So then people try to accommodate each other, don't they, even when anger and unpleasantness come into it?'

He shifted in his chair. Half of him was not even on it.

'Your aggression strengthened me in the belief that I'd made the right decision in not telling you where I was going for the weekend. You would have been furious and wouldn't have accepted it.'

'And then I was furious anyway.'

He said nothing and didn't utter the missing sentence, the one that crossed Ester's mind as a human possibility: that he had always solved this sort of thing by unsentimentally withdrawing. He cut contact. He didn't meet anyone halfway. They had to take what he offered or nothing at all. Inconvenience was not for him. Stimulants that caused discomfort rather than pleasure had to be disposed of. The simplest way to avoid anger was by not concerning yourself with those on whom you had inflicted pain.

'Doesn't she ever get cross?' said Ester.

'Who?'

'The woman in Malmö.'

'I haven't got a woman in Malmö.'

He bit his nails and scanned the street beyond, where freedom lay. Neither of them spoke for a long time. He shifted on the very edge of his seat, leaning forward, about to go. They had not ordered any food, nor would they. Ester hadn't ordered anything at all.

The discomfiture quivered between them.

Then his face lit up as if something witty and entertaining had occurred to him, something he could contribute to the discourse. He said:

'Do you still go running as much as you used to?'

The question was vast in its implications. From it she realized that he did not count her as part of his life in even the slightest way; that she was a hideous distance from him. Her claims and assumptions about an unspoken sense of intellectual fellowship must therefore appear unfathomable to him, not to say mysterious, since his perception of the world was such that he could gaily ask: *Do you still go running as much as you used to?*

It was an attempt to be kind, she realized that. People at great distances from others are often kind. They employ gestures of kindness, which cost nothing. Things that concern other people have little effect on them, so gestures of kindness seem more appropriate than those of malice, which lead only to unpleasantness and trouble. Gestures of kindness mean you will be left in peace.

Hugo Rask was the sort of person who wanted you to think of him as likeable. A warm, considerate man was what he wanted to be. He came across most warmly of all to strangers. The more the strangers got to know him, the cooler and harder he grew.

He drummed on the edge of the table, looking longingly over to his studio.

They stood on the pavement outside the restaurant. He shifted from foot to foot, shuffling restlessly on the spot. Ester ought to go. There would be no more of this tonight, there would be no more of it full stop. She reached out her hand and laid it against his cheek, held it there for a few moments before she lowered her arm, turned and left.

There was snow on the footpath, fresh snow, but well on its way to being slush. She could see in the rear-view mirror of a parked car that he was still standing there, staring after her.

Somewhere within her she knew that the moment a person is not insisting and accusing, resistance becomes meaningless and superiority is transformed into weakness. Disinclination turns into loss, unwillingness into doubt. But not enough of it to make him call her back.

She followed his movements in all the rear-view mirrors, seeing him shake free of his paralysis, walk across the street and enter the building, through the door to the place where he belonged.

In order to seem like a living human being she made an effort to do things, tried to engage in some activity.

She went to Paris.

A good friend of hers had been there for six months for work, and persuaded her to make the trip to revive her spirits and give her something more pleasant to think about. (Interestingly, in general linguistic perception a 'good friend' counts as more distant than a basic 'friend', just as an 'older person' is younger than an old one. This was one of those good friends. More than an acquaintance yet not close.)

She checked into the New Hotel by the Gare du Nord, a claustrophobic little establishment which in case of fire would barely have managed to evacuate its cockroaches. She was allotted a tiny room on the second floor with dust in the corners and a plastic cover on the mattress. The thought of the bodily encounters that had necessitated this arrangement was painful, but no worse than all the other things hacking and stabbing at her internal organs with tools both blunt and sharp. She chewed endlessly over what had happened, with herself and with anyone who

would listen, going through what she could have done differently at such-and-such a time or on such-and-such an
occasion, if only she had known things would turn out as
they had. Not one single step from the moment she and
Hugo went to bed together would she have taken in the
same way, had she known.

One mistake perplexed her. She could not have avoided
it because it arose from a judgement and an evaluation that
she could not consider wrong. The fact that anger was for-
bidden in love was something unknown to her. She could
not conceive that a single outburst of anger, the one she
had sent as a text message on the Saturday evening after
the film, on finding his premises in darkness, was sufficient
to ruin everything. On the contrary, she thought anger was
permitted precisely when you were close to each other.

And perhaps she was right that this was a universally
accepted notion, she thought. And therefore wrong in her
perception of their closeness.

The closeness that makes anger permissible was the
closeness he did not want to have with her.

But why did he want to be physically intimate with her
if he did not want to be close? And why those long, intense
conversations over the preceding months?

She did not understand.

She thought that if she were ever to write a work of
poetry about this she would call it: *Don't understand*.

She had had friendships that had not withstood anger.
They had not been durable, close or loving enough, not of

the type in which fully expressed disappointment was an option; they had lacked the emotional structure to support confrontation. She suspected that this was how their relationship had been for him. He was not attached enough to her to put up with the least amount of bother.

Every morning in her dreary hotel in Paris she made a point of rising at seven and went down to eat breakfast before writing in her room for two hours. She set her alarm and when it rang she stopped work abruptly. Then she went out and walked, moving aimlessly through the city, taking in the atmosphere and the smells. When her legs got tired she went to sit in a cafe and read. For a few minutes here and there it felt as if she was enjoying life and was an individual being who could live without symbiosis. For the rest of the time she was vividly aware that she barely had a life. In those minutes of independence, euphoric in comparison with her general mental state of constant pain, the euphoria made her want to send him a text message to show how independent she was, and happy, how their relationship was based on equality of friendship and how she had accepted things and moved on to new, intrepid goals. She wanted to inform him that she was sitting in a Parisian cafe savouring life and did not need anyone else for mental stimulation because she was strong, thirsty for knowledge, and entirely autonomous.

One day she gave in to the temptation and sent a text. She imagined that the spiritual fellowship she felt inside her was real, and thus mutual. There was no answer, so even those tiny fragments of independence were ruined and the rest of the week was spoilt. Why could she not grasp that the abysmal anguish of an unanswered text was the same every time and the only way to avoid it was not to send any? It was Hope that got her into such a mess, deadening the memory of the shame and anguish and making her take a chance on it all being different this time.

In the evenings she met up with her good friend. They went out for dinner but the good friend did not understand the grief of unrequited love. She thought an unhappy person must be all right if said person produced a laugh or two in the course of an evening. No one seriously burdened down by life could laugh, thought the good friend, who had seen documentaries about chronically depressed people who let their kitchens fester and were given electric shocks. They never laughed. After a disappointment you had to try to move on and remember how well off you were compared to those who were really suffering, people with cancer, the paralysed, the starving and those forced into prostitution. The good friend was not up to carrying others' burdens and wanted everything to be normal so she could take up some space in the conversation for her own troubles and questions without feeling guilty.

After a few evenings they no longer felt like meeting so they saved each other's faces by deciding, wordlessly, discreetly and in total unanimity, to dine alone.

—

Paris was full of smells and fragrances: dirt and buttery pastries, exhaust fumes and perfumes. Day followed day, walk followed walk, impression followed impression and all the while Ester knew it to be a pointless trip. She took in the slender, dark-green metal railings between the pavements and the traffic, the pale-green men who kept the streets clean, all the distinctively Parisian things that she had always loved, and the street corners with their brasseries. Coming to Paris didn't help. Nothing helped if you still had yourself with you.

On her penultimate evening she went out to buy a bottle of wine to go with the takeaway food she planned to eat in her hotel room in front of the television. On the way to the shop, her mobile rang. It was half-past seven. She fished the phone out of her pocket and saw Hugo's name on the display. There it was, plain and clear, Hugo Rask. She stopped in mid-step, stood still and answered with her first name and surname, in a stifled voice. A person with only a first name is sitting there in a flutter, waiting for the world, she thought. First name and surname on the other hand had gravitas, signalled supremacy and self-respect. First name and surname was not waiting pathetically by the phone but was engrossed in something of their own, fully occupied. Surname only would have been even better but, in this context, distancing in such a studied fashion that it would almost sound like a joke. He would be able to see through it.

She let the phone ring several times before answering

and said her first name and surname in a calm, measured tone, then waited to hear his voice. In her ear canals she could hear her heartbeat, but on the line, no one. She could hear the murmur of voices and identified his among them, but none of the voices was talking to her. They were chatting during a break in their work. Someone laughed and someone put down a wine glass on a smooth surface, to judge by the sound an emptied glass and the bar counter in his studio. Was it Eva-Stina's, the one whose name he found hard to remember?

Ester said hello, loudly. After five hellos she stopped. It was at about that point, she sensed, that it could start to seem desperate. Her desperation being real, she was extra-sensitive to the ways desperation could be expressed.

The murmur continued. Receiving calls from Sweden was not free of charge and she would soon have to hang up.

'Hello,' she called, one last time. 'Hello.'

When his name had come up on the display, all hope rushed back, and now she could not rid herself of it. It could not be the case, she argued, that feelings for another person evaporated from one day to the next, and he must have had feelings, otherwise he would not have invested all that time in spending those hours with her. The clear logic of this made it very easy to mobilize hope. All night long she hoped with her whole body, sleeping very little.

The next day was her last one in Paris. She wrote and went out for a walk, sticking to her usual schedule, but breathed in no scents and saw no city. She was consumed by the worry of not knowing whether he had tried to make contact the evening before and had then lost his nerve, or what else it could be. Was he making fun of her? Did he want to make her suffer? For what possible reason?

By the evening she could stand it no longer and called him. The weight that had been constricting her lungs for weeks vanished the moment he answered. He chose to answer, even though he could see it was her. His voice was guarded but when she said she was calling from France it became as soft, warm and enveloping as it had been in their first three months. France was a long way away, as distant as the strangers to whom he was always so warm, and there was no need for him to defend himself.

'You rang me yesterday,' she said, rapt and anxious.

'Did I?' he said amiably.

'Yesterday evening.'

'That's odd.'

'I was on my way to the shop to buy a bottle of wine for my evening meal. I was walking along the pavement in the middle of Paris when you rang. I'm staying near the Gare du Nord. It must have been about half-past seven. But maybe it was by accident?'

'It must have dialled the number itself, in my pocket.'

'There was nobody on the line when I answered.'

They both laughed awkwardly.

'So you're in France?'

You've known this for several days now, she thought, I sent you a text from here on Wednesday, which you didn't answer.

'So it dialled by itself in your pocket?' she said.

'It's always in my pocket. A key must have activated itself when I leant against something.'

'Against the counter in the kitchen.'

'Possibly. Yes, could well have been.'

'You get that sort of thing with these modern devices,' she said.

'Yes, you certainly do,' he said.

'But wasn't it strange that it rang me, of all people? Almost like a sign.'

His laugh was embarrassed now. It generally was, in fact. Ester thought he must find his own laughter uncomfortable because laughter was intimate.

'Maybe your phone's missing me and all those wonderful conversations it listened in on,' she said.

Scornful laughter wasn't intimate, her train of thought continued, but then it wasn't really proper laughter. It merely mimicked the sound and muscle movements of laughter to parasitize the genuine article.

The great expanses of silence in the conversation made her thoughts go bouncing off in various directions.

'Do you remember how lovely it was together? When we talked and talked.'

'Is it all right in France?' he said.

'Yes, fine. Great. Really interesting.'

'France is good,' he said. 'The native land of cheese and wine. And true intellectualism.'

'Paris is always Paris, of course,' she said, feeling the ghastly platitude to be emblematic of their shipwrecked liaison.

'Yes indeed.'

'I've been walking all round the city, soaking up the atmosphere. There's nowhere like it.'

'Sounds splendid.'

'It's spring here. In the capital of love.'

'I can imagine. I mean to say, it's March already. How time flies.'

'Yes. Or creeps by. Anyway, that was all. I just wanted to check whether you rang me yesterday for any particular reason.'

'No. As I said. It must have been an accident.'

'That's a pity.'

She considered the conversation closed and had removed the telephone from her ear when she heard his voice again:

'Maybe speak when you're back, then.'

She put the phone back again.

'What did you say?'

'Maybe speak when you're back, then.'

'Yes? Yes! Shall we? Do let's!'

'OK, we'll do that,' he said. 'Have a nice time until then.'

———

After those small, nonchalant words from his lips she went weightlessly out into the Paris evening, loved every scent and felt in sympathy with every person she saw. She got down to Shakespeare & Company just before they closed and bought a couple of books, one by Hannah Arendt and the other by Derek Parfit, and took an internal decision to work harder, resume her self-discipline, her reading and her efforts to understand how the world fitted together.

She chatted away in bad French to the bookshop assistant while she was paying, and nothing would have the power to annoy her ever again.

It was just before two the following day when her plane landed. Less than an hour later she was back home in her apartment on Kungsholmen. She should probably wait a little while before getting in touch, she thought. It was Sunday, the day when she went for her long-distance training run. She would normally consider a travelling day like this a wasted one for any important activity, but today was another sort of day, it was the start of something new. The biochemical processes that constituted her body were today without obstacles or barriers, nothing was weighing them down or applying any brake. Unresistingly, she went out and did her long Sunday run, even though it was the afternoon. She normally tackled it in the morning or not at all; it often felt too much of an effort to go out later in the day. She was up to eighteen kilometres now, and by the start of May she planned to have increased it to the maximum distance, which she decided would be more than the twenty kilometres she had planned, at least twenty-two. Today, not a single step felt like a struggle. Throughout her circuit, hugging the shoreline of the city's many inlets, she visualized them meeting tonight, and perhaps tomorrow.

He wanted them to be in touch when she got home. And now she was home. Not since the catastrophe occurred had he suggested anything like that. And of course it was no 'accident' that the phone had rung her. It was too improbable. No, he was missing her, too.

After her run she took a bath, with bubbles. Her body was pleasantly tired, particularly her tendons. She felt a sense of satisfaction and inner stability. As soon as she had bathed and dressed she would call him, but not too early, because she had things to do, and a life.

So she took it easy, rubbed herself dry and, still steaming, lay down on the bed to finish sweating and cool down. Ironed a blouse and with it donned a pair of stiff new jeans, some socks she had never worn before and a V-neck jersey of a colour that matched the checked pattern of the blouse.

Her hand did not shake as she made the call, it had no need to. They were to be in touch when she was back from Paris, he had urged her to do it, and now she was home, so she was doing it.

It's too easy to say 'Maybe speak when you're back' with half a continent in between. It's too easy. The content and meaning of the words are too large in relation to how simple they are to utter. No. Wrong track. Like anybody in love, Ester Nilsson laid too much emphasis on the content of the words and their literal meaning and too little on plausibility and her overall judgement. It was part of her profession to assess plausibility and to make overall judgements, and she was good at her profession but that, of course, was an area in which her emotional life was not involved.

Admittedly the content of the sentence he had spoken, 'Maybe speak when you're back,' was not much to go on. It was a standard, polite phrase to someone who was away on a trip. It could mean that you'd be back in touch with each other in a week, or two months. The phrase did not so much express its content as a simple acknowledgement between two people: 'We know each other, we've no scores to settle, this isn't the last time we'll be talking.' But when the phrase was said to someone filled with yearning it was brutal, a sloppy combination of cowardice and guilt, solicitude with nothing behind it.

In her heated state, Ester was unable to see that utterances could be as light as ash and just as burnt-out. They were scattered lazily, fell, came drifting down. Words were not enduring monuments to intentions and truths. They were sounds to fill silences with.

Happiness seldom exists in the experiencing of happiness. It resides in the expectation of happiness and almost only there. Since the evening before, she had been happy.

After what she judged to be eight rings he answered, his voice turned away.

'Hello,' she said. 'It's me.'

His hello was guarded and her voice instantly became strained because her throat constricted and the vocal cords tightened.

'How are you?' she croaked.

'Oh, I'm fine?'

She heard the question mark, its dreadful chill. She sensed a sewer of contempt. He might just as well have come straight out with it: 'Why are you ringing again, don't disturb me, we spoke yesterday, what is it you want of me?'

'I'm doing a bit of work,' he said more mildly, having registered how tense and stifled she suddenly sounded.

'That's good. Working, I mean. I did some work on the plane. Other than that I haven't done much today. It's Sunday, not that that matters, but it's a good excuse if you want a rest.'

She refrained from hanging up abruptly, solely to avoid drawing attention to how ridiculous she felt. She said:

'Going all right?'

'What?'

'Your work.'

'It's going as usual. We've lots to do. We need to get in a good few hours today. The whole team's assembled. We'll be working into the night.'

The freshly ironed blouse clung damply to her back and the inside of her elbows. Don't humiliate me, she thought, I can hear your subtext, I'm not going to gatecrash.

'Did you want anything in particular?' he said.

'No. Nothing in particular.'

He laughed that embarrassed laugh.

'Well, I'm back,' she said.

'Ah yes. Right.'

'I was to call when I got home.'

'Oh yes, you were in Paris.'

'Yes, I was in Paris.'

There was silence for a brief but discernible moment.

'Did you have a good time?'

'No. Because my head and my body came with me.'

He made a sort of humming sound, sensing intimacy in the offing, and wanted to break off. She could hear all she needed to hear to understand definitively that she had to walk away and not spare this man another thought. But the knowledge did not penetrate as far as her autonomous system of insight. It stopped at a more superficial level where excuses feed on whatever they can get hold of. In the never-ending battle between insight and hope, hope won, because insight cost too much to incorporate and hope made it easier to live.

'I wanted to ask if you fancied having dinner,' she said dully.

'Tonight! No, it's impossible!'

They were exclamation marks of sheer dread.

'No, I didn't mean tonight.'

'It's out of the question.'

Shame pulsed at its steady, even pace.

'You said yesterday we should be in touch when I got

home. That was why I called. The only reason. Otherwise I naturally wouldn't have.'

'No problem. I've got to get back to work now. All the best. Bye now.'

Two months passed. It was spring, the season that reveals grimy surfaces and clogged corners. Everything was exposed by the keen rays of the sun. Grief cannot remain acute indefinitely. It soon gets moved to the day ward and then to the rehabilitation clinic. Ester anaesthetized herself with company and people she would not have spent time with had she been harmonious rather than half dead. She did everything in her power to avoid being alone with herself, asking acquaintances and friends to stay over so she could avoid feeling the darkness of the night taking up residence in her.

She was not stoical but in shreds, totally frayed. One evening she decided to ring Per, the man she formerly lived with but had abruptly left six months earlier. She didn't know why she was ringing; her fingers ran ahead of her consciousness. Per said he still loved her, he missed her terribly and everything had been grey since she left. Ester was moved and touched and said she was grateful for the years they had had together. Then Per asked why she was calling and there was something knowing and sharp in his tone. He was as well aware as she was that nothing of that kind happened by chance, it corresponded to internal emotions. Ester said she had just wanted to talk for a while. The next day, Per called twice and asked if perhaps they should try again. On the third day his voice was shrill and he asked what she thought gave her the right to disturb what little equilibrium he had been able to salvage after months of suffering and despair. Ester found it hard to accept she could mean that much to Per, she didn't think it had seemed that way over the years and therefore she didn't really believe him. Moreover she was fully occupied with her own suffering and her own despair. His misery had little genuine effect on her. To her, it seemed unreal.

The girlfriend chorus was kept very busy. It interpreted, comforted, soothed, exhorted and indicated new directions of travel. She had to break free, it said, and she repeated: I've got to break free from this idiocy.

One day, it said, Hugo might turn up at her door with a bunch of flowers, you never knew. But she had to wait until he was ready and be open to life in the meantime.

The girlfriend chorus shouldn't have said that, because she immediately felt the hope of this happening seize hold of her and become the only thing she cared about.

'Do you think it's possible?' she gasped. 'Do you think it could really happen that one day I'll find him at my door and he'll have changed his mind?'

'Everything's possible but you mustn't think about it,' said the chorus.

It was an abortive piece of advice, impossible for her to follow. If there were even the slightest chance, Ester would think of nothing else and live in parenthesis until that day arrived.

Something that had been of crucial importance to her had been nothing but a way of passing the time for Hugo. There were short periods when she dwelt on this thought. Then she deleted it, in order to hold out. In April she wrote two long letters and posted them. She wanted to explain herself and understand. She wanted to put into words what she had felt and why she had acted and thought as she did, wanted to say that his actions had shaped hers, that no one acts without also reacting, that he had given her good cause for making her assumptions.

She did not expect an answer, nor did she get one.

There were days when life was bearable and the pain point shrank to a pinhead.

She read a book about the Holocaust that had just come out, she wrote poems about her misery, which were exceedingly bad but she kept them all the same. She did her five runs a week. Spring progressed. Her legs had clocked up a considerable number of kilometres since the new year.

Towards the end of May she was sitting in a cafe at Östermalmstorg. It wasn't because of its proximity to

Kommendörsgatan that she had ended up there, she persuaded herself. Or rather it was, of course, she conceded. She still gravitated to his district sometimes.

A Christian festival and holiday weekend lasting from Thursday to Sunday was approaching. It was warm and desolate in town. She sat reading over a cup of coffee, able once again to sink into a text, particularly when she was not at home in solitude but, like now, among people and buzz and life. She was in her book, but not so deeply that she missed seeing out of the corner of her eye a coat that she recognized, a shabby green outdoor jacket. There was something about the way the body moved, too, a certain bagginess about both his body and his style. She thought she really must stop seeing him everywhere. Hugo Rask never went to cafes. But here he was now, coming in, approaching her table, raising a hand in greeting and smiling uncertainly.

Ester put down her book on the table, cover uppermost; it was Chekhov's *The Lady With the Dog*. He had once said that she ought to read it. She recalled the moment when she heard him say it and how the warmth between them had felt at that moment of encounter, the way she had been looking out over banks of snow and parked cars as he mentioned the book. Some images just incomprehensibly froze into place. That was six months ago.

Now she was looking out over the paved square, but there was light, there were sap-filled patches of green, what little was planted there plus all the shoots forcing their way through cracks and holes to make their way up to the sun and growth. It was all fresh, nothing past its prime.

Hugo asked how she was, cautiously as if he suspected the answer might have something to do with him, but he evidently wanted to ask anyway. She replied that she was in the final phase of her marathon training. Just the same way as he had used her running in that dreadful way back in February, she used it against him now.

But he wanted to be more intimate and get past the small talk. He sat down, took off his jacket and asked what training in the final phase involved. She didn't think he was interested but answered out of politeness that she went for five runs a week, one of them a two-hour run at an easy pace, the others pushing herself to varying degrees. It was your pulse rate that was important and that morning she had done interval training for forty minutes in total.

He asked why she wanted to run marathons. His eagerness and the way he was enquiring into details felt compensatory; he thought he ought to make an effort, take the initiative. Ester was nonplussed. Their liaison had been rent apart long before and it all seemed rather belated.

But wasn't this what the girlfriend chorus had said, that one day in three months' or three years' time he might turn up at her door with a bunch of flowers and have thought things through properly? Hope took a crazy little leap inside her.

She replied that she ran marathons because it was interesting. There was no other way of finding out or investigating what happened to your body and head after thirty kilometres and then after thirty-five. It was a sort of study.

Hugo said that as studies went, it sounded taxing. To him, the dividend seemed hard-earned and negligible.

'But clearly I don't think so,' she said. 'Since I do it.'

His coffee came. He nodded his thanks.

'I didn't really mean to come in here. But I saw you sitting here, so I did.'

She put Chekhov in her bag.

'Is it as good as I remember it?' he said.

'Very good. Exceptional, in fact.'

'Thank you for your letters,' he said. 'They were sensitive, elegant.'

'Do you think so?'

'One of them was simply beautiful.'

The other one had contained some reproaches in the form of questions interspersed with the tokens of love.

'I don't remember what I wrote,' she said. 'It was a long time ago.'

'Sorry I didn't answer them.'

'Are you?'

'I should've answered. But I've had so much work on all spring. And it isn't over yet.'

She could sense the effort it took for him to say that. And she realized he wanted absolution from his guilt because he had extended a hand, and that he now thought it up to her to grant it to him. She had never known any-body, in fact, who had admitted their guilt and also been able to bear it.

Well-dressed people crossed the square with foodie treats for the weekend in bags from the Östermalmshallen market.

Ester would not allow him to discharge his debt by playing down the pain his actions and lack of replies had caused her. She resisted hard when the reflex action of making things easy for him tried to kick in. Having not offered him the relief he sought, she fully expected some kind of accusation or spiteful comment to follow.

And it did. He said:

'You knew I was seeing another woman.'

'No. I didn't know. You never told me about her and you denied it when I asked. It was no thanks to you I managed to work out that she existed. And naturally I thought you'd left her when you came to me. I thought that was why you came then rather than earlier. I thought you were waiting to settle old business. I thought that was what one did unless one was a bigamist. It's OK being a bigamist of course, but you have to make it clear. But until further notice, one at a time is presumably the implicit ground rule.'

'But that would mean breaking up!'

'Yes?'

'But that's so awkward and such a hassle.'

He sounded genuinely perplexed.

'Well the alternative turned out pretty awkward and bothersome too, for me.'

'All this having to talk about everything and be honest and transparent, it's only a convention,' he said. 'A suffocating totalitarian imposition, a restriction we inflict on one another. To demand that a person with whom one has had physical contact give up everything from that moment on is tyranny. To demand that, after this physical contact, he never again be allowed to keep anything for himself is not only petty bourgeois, but also indicates a total lack of respect for the freedom of the individual, which you generally esteem so highly.'

Ester found that it hurt both to blink and to swallow.

'I can't contradict you,' she said. 'Unfortunately.'

'Must be the first time.'

He laughed. But she didn't.

'I can't contradict you in any way except to say that one party's freedom is sometimes the other's distress.'

It was a lovely afternoon, the kind you only get in May. The wind caressed the sun umbrellas, making the fabric ripple indolently; it was warm, almost hot, yet still fresh as it breezed in through the open window. The weather was pleasant enough to sit outside but Ester preferred both eating and reading indoors.

'Who is she?'

'Who?'

'The woman you meet up with as regularly as clockwork but conceal and never talk about?'

'We've known each other decades.'

'What does she do?'

'Teach. History and social sciences.'

'Secondary level?'

'Upper secondary.'

'She lives a long way from here?'

'It's nice to get away.'

'To hide from everything and everyone. Have a secret life so you can keep everyone at a mental distance, even her. If you have more than one woman, or man, you need never be really close to anyone. Never be on equal terms, never lay yourself open to anything, you can manipulate power so you never end up the subordinate but have always got someone else to go to. A sort of existential hedging of bets.'

'I like it on the train.'

'A person who starts lying about the little things is soon lying about everything, about his whole life. And is forced to live behind a screen.'

'I'm not lying. Not telling the whole story isn't lying.'

'Don't you want to live with her properly?'

'She wants that. Wants me to move down there with her.'

'But you don't?'

'When I'm eighty perhaps.'

'Does she know you've got other women?'

'I'm sure she does.'

'I'm not, unless you've actually talked about it. People don't. There's no way of knowing. You ought to tell her.'

'Why hurt people?'

He stroked his chin, starting from his cheeks, and it made a rasping sound.

'What were you imagining when you just gave up on me last winter, overnight?'

'You've got your life ahead of you,' said Hugo. 'I haven't.'

The age difference, well, it was a valid argument she supposed, and the only one she could not do anything about. It was the first explanation he had given her that was the result of some reflection.

For a very brief space of time she had a presentiment that one day she would be thoroughly tired of this story and indifferent to its outcome. She sensed that she would look back in amazement on her struggle and the fact that she had thought him worth it. And on that day she would thank her lucky stars at having escaped his company. It was a fleeting thought among others. She found him pitiful, planted there so heavily on his chair, admitting his own vulgarity, his cheerless life and his fear, which he attempted to ennoble into broad-mindedness.

Two women sat down at the empty table next to them. One of them was telling a story and the other was laughing loudly, lapsing into silence for the next bit and then bursting out laughing again. The one talking seemed satisfied with the merriment but embarrassed by the shrillness of the laugh, trying to get her companion to tone it down by speaking more mutedly herself.

Ester and Hugo looked at the women.

'You never laugh like that when I tell you something,' he said.

He stroked Ester's arm and she felt the beating of her heart.

'I've never had reason to,' she said.

'Mm, because we have a more serious relationship.'

He looked at her, clear-eyed and with no ulterior motive. One of the cafe staff wiped a table, another placed an espresso in front of a woman in a suit, who unfolded a copy of the *Financial Times*.

'We haven't got a relationship, have we?'

'But we're serious. We would have a serious relationship if we did have one. And anyway, we *have* laughed together, a lot.'

'Yes we have, actually.'

The only weapon of someone who loves is to stop loving. However messy and demanding their love may have seemed to its object, it goes against the grain to be deprived of it, even though the object may never have wanted it in the first place. It is the balance of power that is shifted by the new indifference, and the fear of appearing foolish and ordinary in the eyes of the one who formerly did the loving.

'Do you remember that time we were round at my place last winter?' she said.

'Of course I do.'

'Do you remember what we had to eat?'

'You served chicken. In a creamy sauce.'

'Crème fraiche with white wine and Gruyère cheese.'

'Not all that many plants in there.'

He made a self-satisfied little sound. She noted the way he was deliberately reeling her in by means of those precise little references to their shared past, and was glad.

'It had a reddish colour.'

'There was paprika in it,' she said. 'How interesting, you remember with your eyes. You really are a visual artist through and through. I remember with my ears, and with my eyes only if they see the printed word. And a few other body parts, I remember with those as well.'

His jacket, way too warm for the season, was on again because they were about to go. The fact that he had taken it off was all part of the effort and compensation for all the coats previously left unremoved, she thought.

'I don't only remember with my eyes, either,' he said.

Don't do this, thought Ester. Don't drag me into this again. I'm just starting to break free.

But she loved the way his eyes glistened when he was talking about memories of their encounters and she felt very close to him.

'It was paprika that made it look red,' she said again.

'It was delicious. Didn't I bring a chair with me, too? Have you still got it?'

'I sit on it every day.'

'Well it's good to know I made some kind of contribution, at least.'

'I've never understood why you went to bed with me three times after months of prevarication and then just disappeared. I've never understood how you could do that, and why you would never talk to me about it when I asked you to.'

He averted his head and his gaze followed a decrepit couple who were walking very slowly, supporting each other.

'There's no point my trying to explain. You already know the answer to all my questions and you've got all your objections ready.'

'It's a shame you see it that way. I'm very curious to hear your thoughts on the subject and I'd really like to hear your version. But maybe I interpret events differently from you. And maybe that's what you want to spare yourself?'

They were standing in Östermalmstorg, down by the turning area where Humlegårdsgatan meets Nybrogatan. She held out her hand as if for a handshake. They had never shaken hands since the first time they met, back in October. With some hesitation he took her hand, since the gesture had something distanced and final about it.

He made sure they were looking each other in the eye and said:

'I shall really think about this, Ester. This you and me thing, us.'

She heard him say it. She didn't mishear. She wanted to ask him to repeat it and wished she had recorded it, but she hadn't imagined it. She had heard correctly.

'What did you say?'

He looked at his watch. It was time to part. He had to

get back to his life and she to her non-life. With it being a long weekend, she presumed he would be making the trip to see his woman.

'I'm just going to the off-licence,' he said. 'Come with me.'

She thought: This is the time to walk away and not look back.

She went with him to the off-licence. It was very busy. While they were waiting for his turn in the queue she asked what he was doing this weekend; it extended over four days.

He said he was going up to Borås.

It could be stupidity or a pure reflex action that made him resort to that fib again after he had just told her about the woman down in Malmö. But Ester thought: What he's telling me now is that I needn't imagine that other relationship is hugely important; that there's a chance and I should hold on and wait.

She did not think of the way one can lie out of respect, misjudged but humane, of the way – out of fear of the other's anguish and insistent dependence – one can say lots of things one doesn't mean, to be kind, to spare a tormented individual from the brutal insight of how she is rated, and from the self-evident fact that one does not want that other person near, not in the way she wants. Nor did she think that he was saying what he said because it is disagreeable to talk of one's intentions and actions in front of people who offer silent or explicitly moral verdicts on everything, based on emotions and justified by that exacting weakness, and then to have to supply a volley of common-sense reasons for them.

'I shall go to Leksand as well,' he added, and it sounded like a relief to him to be able to say it.

The queue numbers ticked forward. She wondered which observations it would be wise to refrain from just now. This was how he had talked at the beginning of their association, Leksand, Borås, as if the travelling itself would impress her, make him seem exciting and independent, as if such places drew attention to the absence of awkward ties in his life by conveying how freely he travelled, and alone. He was like a child who by saying 'Leksand, Borås' instead of 'Malmö, banal relationship' believed himself to be saying: I haven't done anything! I'm innocent!

'How are you going to get between Borås and Leksand quickly enough to be able to spend time in them both?'

'By train.'

The house in Leksand was the symbol of his autonomy. He had been there alone when he needed to find himself, and when there he was not linked to any woman. He knew that she knew it. It represented his dream of getting by without the power of women over him. It had happened before that he had gone off to Leksand to show how free and unfettered he was. Why had he done it? Perhaps because she made him see his situation from her own severe point of view and realize that he was ridiculous. Had this struck her she would have approved, for she had been wronged and her point of view was therefore the right one.

What she missed was that even if her view of the matter was the most reasonable it was not perceived as such, but only as a sign of rigid irreproachability. Which generates shame, which leads to lies. People lie to be free. People lie because they will not be left in peace if they tell it the way it is. People lie because other people assume the right to confront them in the name of truth. Lying as an escape from irreproachability turns into an act of resistance to an honesty with totalitarian expectations. Ester Nilsson would have seen that, if only she had not been so involved in the story herself. It was so entwined with pain and disappointment that certain observations were bound to be overshadowed by her own empirical evidence.

For some, lying is also an addiction, with all the components of an addiction. Hugo Rask could not resist telling untruths if he got the chance, in order to avoid being the object of loving individuals' entire catalogue of rights and programme of reforms, in order to hide from the eyes of the world, which he both craved and could not endure.

But maybe it would be asking too much of Ester in this situation to realize that he said what he said not because he was wavering, but so that she would not think him pathetic. All Ester heard was that he had just said something unprecedented, namely that he would think through their relationship, that he might want to be with her, that the age difference had been the only hurdle. In other words, that there had not been anything wrong with the relationship or with her.

She stood in the off-licence in Nybrogatan with Hugo, wishing that his number would never tick onto the screen. She would have liked to stand there for the rest of her life, and then she heard him say something even more unprecedented.

'I'll show you Leksand sometime.'

There was a roaring in her head. His gaze met hers, naked, pure and sincere. Then it was his turn to be served. He bought four bottles of red. They went to his studio and at the entrance they embraced and said goodbye.

Then Ester walked all the way home. She could have walked a hundred kilometres that evening. The pavements were drenched in saturated afternoon sun, rich in promise with summer on the doorstep. 'I'll show you Leksand sometime,' she heard over and over again. 'I'll show you Leksand sometime.'

He couldn't make such pledges without meaning something by them. It was impossible.

However, the new possibility that had opened up only took the form of more waiting. She wanted to get her life going, get it going right away, but she was left waiting again.

Love, the real big thing, was a battle and an intoxication, that was how she accounted to the sceptical for this relationship being so complicated and demanding, and bringing her only suffering and no joy. The girlfriend chorus sometimes contradicted her, saying love was harmony and that you were considerate to each other, not this endless toil she felt obliged to engage in.

People who said that didn't understand. The harmony would come once she had toiled for it. You had to earn it. You had to suffer and struggle in order for pleasure to arrive and then be worth something.

After the weekend she called him, even though she had intended to wait until he rang. She managed to hold off for a day, the Monday, but no longer. He answered quickly in a happy, or cheerful, voice. Again it was the ingratiating, obliging voice of a child that wanted to show it had done everything right and not told any lies.

Hugo said the sun had been shining in Leksand.

Perhaps it had, she thought, but not on him.

The crucial thing for her interpretation of events, however, was noting that he still seemed to be in the same state of mind as when they met a few days previously. He was not dismissive and surly. He still seemed at pains to play down the other liaison by talking about Leksand. That meant he was not standing by his woman, calculated Ester, which in turn meant he did not love her but was open to other options, she also calculated, which meant that he had not made up his mind, which meant there was a chance and that it was a substantial one.

It did not strike her that disloyalty could be a character trait and that whoever was at his side would be exposed to it. With Ester, it would all be different.

He asked whether she had done much running over the weekend and she replied that she had run forty kilometres since they last met. Her training still lay like something semi-permeable between them, a prerequisite for, yet a barrier to, their proximity.

'That's a whole marathon!' he exclaimed.

'But spread over three sessions,' she said.

Why was she ringing him today? Because she hoped for an answer to the deliberations he had promised to undertake? Not really. That wasn't realistic. She was ringing because the itch was back, the malarial love itch that is always latent once it has invaded the cell system, lying ready to break out at any time.

The mood that had gradually developed through the spring, in which she had finally resigned herself and stopped thinking in terms of tactical manoeuvres, no longer counting the hours of nobly restraining herself from making that call, evaporated in the half hour their meeting in the cafe lasted. When the brain perceives contact as possible, every hour is too long. That is the state of enslavement. The state in which the prospect of intoxication takes over the organism.

So why was she ringing him today?

To be in contact. She thought she had better give some reason for seeking that contact and asked whether he felt he could make some kind of judgement . . . preliminary of course . . . she realized he couldn't know . . . but perhaps just a rough idea . . . a cautious estimate . . . of how long he needed to think about it?

She wondered whether she could invite him to her apartment again, maybe fish this time, zander perhaps, with riced potatoes and a green salad dressed with a good olive oil, plus a dry wine to go with it. Then coffee and chocolate cake, not ice cream but a succulent chocolate cake with a high cocoa content that she'd make herself. Or would a chocolate mousse be more elegant than a chocolate cake? And what was best to follow fish? There were particular rules and regulations for things like that, heavy as a counterpoint to light, sour contrasting with sweet.

She heard a hesitant cough, and then he said:

'Think about what?'

There was no sarcasm in the question. He didn't know what she was talking about.

'You were going to think about you and me.'

She could hear the neurons firing in his cerebral cortex as he searched his memory. Then he found what he sought and said:

'It's not something one can think over that quickly. That kind of thing takes time, you know.'

Of all the comments he could have made this was the worst, because everything in existence wants to live and hope is no exception. It is a parasite. It lives and thrives on the most innocent of tissue. Its survival lies in a well-developed ability to ignore everything that is not favourable to its growth while pouncing on anything that will feed it and help it to live on. Then it ruminates on these crumbs until every trace of nourishment has been extracted from them. Now hope was gnawing with divine frenzy. For a few short seconds she was weightless.

'I'll give you all the time you need,' she said, but had no time to finish her sentence before he cried out:

'Ohhh! A bird just flew into the window here. Nasty. I think it's broken its neck.'

She heard his chair scrape.

'Nature's so brutal! Poor bird. I'd better deal with it. It's lying here in pain, cheeping.'

Ester could visualize the bird. It must be lying outside on the narrow metal window sill that was just a few centimetres wide. It seemed a physical impossibility for it to have fallen straight down and, what was more, not toppled over the edge if it had been flying at such speed as to injure itself so badly. But perhaps it had happened some other way.

She wondered how the bird could have chosen such an inconvenient moment.

'It'll soon be summer,' she said. 'You'll be going away I expect?'

'Yes, it's summer now,' he said, making it sound like something inherently wonderful.

'I loathe summer,' Ester said.

'I'm not surprised. You're so critical of everything other people like.'

'I do seem to have the best of reasons for that.'

She rang off. They had no contact for months.

After the marathon, the first weekend in June, she felt such a strong urge to send him her finishing time, 3.45.27. That and nothing else. And maybe also 27°. And maybe also: 'Legs ache.' And maybe also: 'Do you want to meet up this week?'

She wrote it all, then deleted it.

Every day she made the bed. She had read that this indicated inner stability. Then she lay on top of the covers in her hot apartment while the hours accumulated. Through the permanently open windows she could hear the summer sounds of the wasps, flies and seagulls.

She forced herself to work but had nothing to say.

An acquaintance had suggested she read Mayakovsky's correspondence with Lili Brik. She read it and saw that everybody loved and wept in the same way and for much the same reasons, everybody betrayed and was betrayed in the same way and everybody thought: No one has ever loved like this before or suffered such agony. Everybody was unique in the same way. In every time and every place.

Sections of the girlfriend chorus were irritated when she told them about this Russian consolation and said she seemed to think she was finer, grander and more sensitive in her pain.

'It's kind of like, you and the Poets. But every heart has its tale to tell, don't go thinking you can love more than all the rest.'

She found this misunderstanding hurtful because the

insight Brik and Mayakovsky had given her was just the opposite, that she was not alone and her pain was not special. And besides, she was a poet herself. It was unpleasant not to be understood by your close friends but to be rebuked as conceited. When she wanted to share her enthusiasm about something she had read and thought she could do this with the notion of absolute trust, because she felt at ease with the person she was talking to and not obliged to crop all the bits that stuck out and flopped over the sides, not thinking that these could be used against her.

But she had to learn that you could not let anybody see the full picture of what was going on inside you. Trust like that did not exist. Everyone had a cranny in which scepticism and distaste could lurk, a secret aversion nurtured by anxious supervision, envy and common-or-garden rancour, in which they stored away all their thoughts as they listened to the most candid of confessions.

You had to love a person tremendously to tolerate her hunger.

Ester often went to the cinema that summer. Fled to the temple of those who were too timid for life, the domain of the troglodytes. One afternoon she saw Kurosawa's *The Seven Samurai*. Afterwards she wanted to talk to Hugo about it. She wanted to talk to Hugo about everything but particularly this film, which he claimed in an interview to have been deeply influenced by.

But he was down in Europe somewhere with his woman.

They headed south for the summer. He went to look at battle sites from one of the world wars. He was interested in that sort of thing: scenes of action, ruins and cemeteries. He photographed them, drew them, let them give him impulses for pictures and suggest moral stances on the theme of power and violence. Anything that spoke of all that was brutal and lamentable about human beings, plus that little gesture of warmth in the shadow of the brutality, stimulated him even more.

Ester emerged from the darkness of the cinema and walked home in the never-ebbing sun. Pouring down, burning, it stabbed at her eyes and made her long to be cool. She hated the sun because it was so hot, because it showed no humility in the face of its own resources and her dependence on them, because it was indifferent to whether she lived or died from its goddamned rays.

And then, from one day to the next, a new sound came into the leaves, a forgotten nip into the air. It was autumn sending out an experimental feeler. Finally, licentious summer shaded into the time of disciplining and retreat, the time when the harmonious would return from their summer sojourns and the lonely become less lonely.

Ester allowed a bohemian new acquaintance from Boston with nowhere to live to camp in her kitchen for a while. He was an art critic and had written an extended and erudite essay on Hugo Rask. That was how they met. She sought him out at the university after the summer to ask him a few questions and it turned out that he needed some accommodation. If she couldn't have Hugo with her, someone who knew about his art would have to do instead. They talked for hours, every day. She bought a two-person coffee machine and wondered whether they could go to bed together. But she soon asked the American to move out. She couldn't bear being observed all the time, never left alone with her thoughts. Every morning he occupied her bathroom for an hour. In the end she couldn't stop herself shouting that she had to be alone and why didn't he find a flat through that network of contacts he was always boasting about. He moved out the same day.

Hugo and Ester had not been in touch since a bird broke its neck by crashing into his window on one of the last days in May.

At the end of September, an email arrived.

An email arrived from Hugo Rask.

Four months after they had last spoken, there was an email from Hugo Rask in her inbox.

She had been convinced they would never be in touch again.

She was ecstatic at simply seeing his name and thought she must have made a mistake and it was an old email playing tricks on her.

What could Hugo be writing to Ester after that long silence? He wrote that he had thought of her when he read an article in the paper the other day and that he had had an operation to remove the meniscus in his knee.

The knee, their shared body part, the one she had been allowed to touch before she was allowed to hold the rest of him. It was not fraught with danger but sufficiently erotic for him to use the reference to lasso her now. Every time they met in the early winter she had asked how his knee was, and felt it under the table to make a diagnosis. Repetitive stress disorder was her special subject.

He also wrote a line about the recent general election and deplored the outcome, reported that he had been in a hard and intense period of work recently and had not been able to be sociable for a long time.

So would they have met, otherwise? Was that what he intended to say? Or did he mean that she was not the only one he never met, he hadn't time for any socializing at all and she shouldn't feel she'd been replaced or ousted?

He did not propose any meeting.

Ester wondered what had prompted him to get in touch. The only thing she could think of was that a human rights organization on whose committee she sat had approached him to propose a collaborative venture. She had kept quiet at the meetings where they had talked about Hugo's important work on issues relating to human rights and the desirability of involving him in their new project. He agreed to a meeting and the other committee members asked Ester to be part of it because they knew she had given a lecture on Hugo the previous autumn and admired his art and his courage. She had declined. Hugo knew she was on that committee. The meeting had been yesterday. He had noted her absence of course, and wondered about it.

The dynamics were as regulated by laws as the motion of the tides, and had the same origins.

But the urge to be worshipped without the wish to love in return was something Ester found so strange that she had to assume his contact-seeking after the discovery that she was avoiding him was a sign that he missed her. Otherwise she did not understand what he was up to.

The horrific possibility presented itself that he only wanted to be assured of her continuing goodwill. But it got no purchase on her. She could not go so far as to see things in that cynical light, even though she had observed that he always wanted to show his most genial face to the world, because the world was potentially hostile. The world was all that was Other, and that made her the world, so she had to be disarmed just in case she was honing a weapon. The world was always honing weapons. Rather than forfeit the love and admiration that kept her faithfully placid, thus setting them both free, he tossed her yet another juicy bone – and consigned her once again to the mincer.

Forgoing the gestures of lazy concern.

Being strong enough to wear the mask of cruelty.

Amputating the leg that will otherwise rot from gangrene.

These were not for him.

She waited twenty-four hours to reply. It took her two hours to compress it down into five lines. The message that resulted from all this painstaking effort was controlled and reserved but sufficiently affirmative and full of melancholy yearning to ensure he would not be back in touch.

He would receive all the confirmation he needed and could go quiet again.

A fleeting whiff of something wonderful is harder to bear than nothing at all. Hugo's re-entry into her existence sabotaged in a few seconds her months of work on alleviating her symptoms. The itch was back and she started trying to reach him anew, convinced that nothing comes to anyone who fails to make an effort. And he answered. Everything intensified and came flooding back. Whatever had been lying at rest in her body arose intact and resumed its dominion. The hours once again grew long and full of waiting, and everything besides contact with him was meaningless, which meant that most things were meaningless because the contact was scanty and sporadic.

The girlfriend chorus said: Too much time's gone by. If he wanted anything with you he'd show it.

Ester turned her back on the chorus. It did not understand.

Once in the course of the autumn he said he was going to call so they could decide on a date to meet. The call never came. When she rang him he said it was a good job she'd got in touch because he had lost her number in his most recent change of mobile phone. She sent a letter on paper in which she wondered why he kept making contact and holding out the prospect of things when he never lived up to them. No reply.

She could see with crystalline clarity that her behaviour was absurd, and put the blame on him: if only he had not got in touch in that futile way in September, if only he had left her in peace. It is the stronger party, the one who wants least, who has to hold their impulses in check, she told the girlfriend chorus when it enquired why she didn't concentrate on her own behaviour rather than his; after all, she knew everything she needed to know about him. She couldn't change him, only herself etc.

'It would take less for him to change than for me, because he wants nothing,' Ester said. 'He's the one who has to impose some self-discipline, not me, because I want something different to happen from what is, you see. It costs him nothing, not getting in touch. Whereas it costs me the risk of missing that microscopic chance.'

But surely you don't believe in miracles? said the girlfriend chorus.

She convinced herself and others that she was no longer hoping the two of them would become a couple. All she wanted was an admission – of what had been, that there had been something, that he had felt something, that there had been times when he doubted and wavered – and for him to have got back in touch this autumn in spite of it all being over because there was a damp patch in him that refused to dry.

When nothing else remains, there's redress to fight for, so that one can continue the struggle and not sink into resignation. Even redress requires contact. If she could only purge herself of that longing for contact. That's what was hollowing her out. If only she could become indifferent to him.

She thought about the amazing fact that seven billion people on earth did not have this reliance on hearing from him. Their health and wellbeing did not depend on it. So why did hers? There was no rhyme or reason to it. Why could she not feel the same towards him as the seven billion did, living their lives with complete lack of concern for what he was engaged in?

The girlfriend chorus said: Give up and leave this man. He's doing you harm.

The girlfriend chorus really didn't understand. They were the seven billion.

November came and a documentary film was being made about Hugo Rask. It was almost finished. He invited her in to an advance screening so she could express her opinions on the film. He needed her 'critical eye and sharp brain', as he put it, for there was still time to do some re-cutting of the film.

Off she went, pleased by his praise but even more pleased that she would get to see him. It was the first time in six months, the first time since they had coffee in the cafe on the square and he had said he was going to show her Leksand.

The film studio was in Bergsgatan at street level, a poky venue with shabby décor and fluorescent strip lighting on the ceiling. She had made her way there on foot in good time, so in order not to be the first to arrive she stationed herself on a street corner with a view of the entrance. Once a number of people had arrived she went to the door. The audience largely comprised his customary garland of hangers-on, the whole entourage of unpaid interns from the art schools who worked for him in the hope that a stroke from his paintbrush of genius would touch their souls.

The lights went down and the film started. It was about an hour long and followed him through all the various stages of his work, and through interviews in which he expounded his world view. She had heard it before, the same examples and anecdotes that he usually employed, which from her reading she knew him to have used twenty years before. No variation, no movement. His head appeared to have petrified at a high level and got stuck there.

Once the film was over, they were all asked to share their individual thoughts. To Ester's consternation, no one had anything critical to say about what they had seen, or even an interesting reflection. She did not understand this homage. The film was utterly pointless, unpolished and lacking any narrative thread, conceivably acceptable as an early draft and, in the way of early drafts, without the depth that only comes from the sediment gradually accruing from a work that has been allowed to take its time. This was a rushed piece of work. Moreover, the film was embarrassingly deferential.

As she sat there listening to their mechanical, cultish adoration she thought that the others, those who were part of his staff, worshipped him – but she loved him. A person who loved did not need to adore. For the worshipper, the object had to be kept intact in order not to split apart if flaws were discovered. The lover, by contrast, was free to judge. She loved him even when the element deserving of worship disappeared, in fact more so then, for she loved his person, not his work. And wasn't that what the editor of the philosophical periodical *The Cave* had meant exactly a year ago, although Ester had not fully appreciated it?

It was Ester's turn to speak and her first question was mild and exploratory, for she did not want to appear brusque: Had the idea been to make a PR film about him in preparation for the forthcoming exhibitions in Tokyo and Turin? Hugo's expression shifted towards vulnerability, and he said he had had nothing to do with the production side. The film was supposed to be a penetrating and objective documentary. Ester said nothing as she wondered how to approach what she felt she had to say.

'It feels terribly uncritical,' she said.

'Why should it be critical?' said one of his staff.

'Exactly. Why do we always have to find fault?' said someone else.

'Naturally it doesn't have to be critical in a negative sense,' said Ester, 'or even supposedly objective. But it does have to be testing, neutral, searching and unprejudiced, prepared to disturb the viewers' habitual lazy thinking. This film already knows what it wants when the filming starts and uses the same phrases that are always used about Hugo. It isn't trying to discover anything; it just wants to confirm what we already think.'

'And what do we think?'

The question was asked irritably from among the cabin stewards and refuse collectors of his mind, those who had been assigned to, and taken as their mission, the task of defending the object of their worship from hearing the truth, which he in his turn was allegedly seeking.

Ester thought he wanted adoring people around him, that was what he wanted and made sure to get, showing them what was expected of them. He did not want her 'critical eye and sharp brain' in either his love life or his professional life. She had been allowed to be near him as long as she did not see him for what he was.

'The film wants to pay homage,' she said. 'It wants us to worship its subject.'

'Deservingly, do you mean?' said the staff.

'It makes no odds whether it's deserved or undeserved. Homage isn't interesting. One wants to learn something, get some depth, problem solving, interpretation. Not a panegyric.'

Only now did it strike her that it was Eva-Stina who had

asked the most acerbic questions. She had changed her glasses and hairstyle since last winter, perhaps even had her hair tinted a different shade. She was sitting along-side Hugo, sitting awfully close to him and glowering infernally, except when she was yawning at the trivialities being aired.

'The film was good,' Ester said. 'I need to see it again, of course, to be able to assess it properly.'

The session ended and the whole group went out for a meal at a little local restaurant. Some of them seemed to feel that it had been a case of freezing out in the viewing studio and were extra solicitous to Ester while they waited for the food, solicitous in that pitying, patronizing way adopted by convinced but tolerant people when the gulf is too great. Kindly beings who have seen the light and are eager in their attentions because their horror at the deviant's lack of judgement would be ugly and harsh if they let it show. They smiled sect-like smiles and asked how familiar she was with the craft of documentary film-making. She smiled back, as fearful as they were, and replied that her particular interest was the mechanisms of oppression and the adulation of leaders in totalitarian systems rather than documentary films. They ignored her remark and insisted with warm smiles on knowing more about her ignorance of the documentary film's particular requirements and aesthetic.

They ate and drank, and when it was time to go home Hugo Rask stood on the pavement under the pale light of a shop sign. He stood there with Dragan, who had been regarding Ester with reluctant interest when she made critical comments on the film. Ester could see by the way he looked that he agreed with her. On the other side of Hugo stood Eva-Stina with her hands in her pockets and her hair curling out from under her hat. In a way that Ester could not quite put her finger on, they appeared to find it natural for Eva-Stina to be there beside them.

It had just been raining. The asphalt was a dark mirror in which they could see themselves and others.

The autumn passed, the days rambled by, the hours moving more quickly now that Ester Nilsson had given up hope again. Since the screening of the documentary there had been silence.

A few days before Christmas she went to a party, a big occasion to which everyone who had commented publicly on the cultural climate of the land was invited. She was idly stirring the almonds and raisins served with the *glögg* when she saw him standing over by the wall, without company. It had not occurred to her that he might have been invited – it was mainly journalists, academics and writers. He met her gaze and held it.

The floor space was crowded for they were many, the commentators on the society in which they lived, a multitude of like-minded anti-conformists, most of them on their way to a more exciting party somewhere else. People came and joined him and exchanged a few words with him before sliding on to the next conversation. Ester tried to be discreet in her attention but noted that he was as aware of her position in the room as she was of his. Not wanting to let this show made him look shifty, his eyes never still.

It was one of those parties where you were expected to stand, your plate in your hand with the wineglass fixed in a plastic holder. Her insides had turned to shapeless softness within seconds. She was thankful for all those times lately when she had resisted the temptation to inform him of her utter contempt. Self-control was something one almost never had call to regret. Anger and outbursts were things one almost always wished undone. The tricky part was to know exactly where one stood in the segment between 'almost never' and 'almost always', when the angry outburst was justified and produced the most favourable result.

Ester went across to him.

They did not embrace as others around them were doing. She thought that was a good sign; their bodies still had some kind of electric charge. She sensed in the furthest regions of her consciousness that the fact that she still thought in signs was not good, and had to be seen as symbolic of her lack of freedom. He was leaning back slightly and doing that glinting thing with his eyes. He popped an olive in his mouth.

'Nice olives they've got here,' he said. 'Not out of a jar.'

'I didn't think you came to this sort of event,' she said.

'I don't. But they nagged.'

He looked away.

As a sign: not good.

'Did you think I'd be here?' she asked.

'The question didn't cross my mind.'

As a sign: bad, but the indifference could equally well be feigned with some difficulty and mean the opposite.

'Do you like this sort of food?'

He surveyed his plate as if seeing it for the first time.

'Isn't it just the same old oily antipasti as usual?'

He was making a joke: promising.

She laughed loudly and his face brightened: good. The guarded expression faded: very good. But he also shifted his weight to the other leg and looked around the room in a way that: less good, bore witness to his being uncomfortable and not wanting to stand there with her: terrible, he was looking for a reason to go, looking for an escape route: disaster.

The girlfriend chorus had taken up residence in her head and now said: But can't you see he doesn't want to, you've not been together for nearly a year. What are you doing?

She thought: I should walk away. But I don't want to. I want to stand here with him. It's the only place in the world I want to be.

The girlfriend chorus said: Where's your pride?

She answered: I have no pride because pride is linked to shame and honour, and I'm shameless and have no concept of what others find honourable.

The chorus said: That's what constitutes your pride, showing how free you are from the things that fetter more conformist souls. Deep inside you're a snobbish intellectual.

There was a group of people standing a little way from them, talking about the USA's latest war of aggression. Admittedly it was a dreadful regime over there, they said, but they would have done better to support the underground democracy movements instead. Hugo Rask was looking at them.

'Is it any nicer to be blown to smithereens by a bomb if the person dropping it has been sent by a democratically elected government?' said Ester Nilsson.

'What?'

'I think I'm a pacifist, actually. I've reached the conclusion that it's for the best in the long run. Even if it means being invaded, occupied, deprived of one's liberty, taken into slavery. One shouldn't fight, just give in. Throw the hydrogen bombs into the sea, as Olof Lagercrantz wrote. Just decide violence is never permissible. Otherwise one's stuck with endless assessments of potential consequences, and there's no way of getting it right.'

He nodded, but in the wrong places. Even as a pacifist she was of no interest to him.

He drank his wine in embarrassed gulps. The group discussing the latest American war of aggression was hearing the opposing view put forward by a refugee from the country on the receiving end of the strikes, who had made his name as a leader writer and now said the only sensible course of action was to bomb his stupid countrymen to bits because they knew no better.

Hugo glanced sideways at Ester to see what she thought.

But she also saw that he could not really be bothered to listen to what she thought, on that or any other subject. He was shifting jarringly from foot to foot.

'Refugee status doesn't automatically confer reasonable opinions,' said Ester.

'There are lots of people here,' said Hugo.

'Yes.'

'The whole cultural mafia.'

'Yes, all of them, and then us,' she said with dry self-deprecation and took her eyes off him for the first time, which immediately made him more alert and attentive.

'But don't you think some people count themselves part of it as a matter of course? We are a bit odd, you and I, when all's said and done.'

The furthest regions of her consciousness: a kinship comment, generated by the suggestion of her resignation. He had reacted immediately to the distancing. That was the way it had been all along, she thought in some stab at self-defence, and that was why she was caught in his net.

'Everyone likes swimming against the tide,' said Ester. 'That's what the tide is.'

'Perhaps it's the human condition,' he said.

'Presumably. Or one of them.'

She prepared to move off round the room.

'I saw a book I thought of buying for you,' he said.

For fear that he might regret it, she rendered her face immobile.

'Where?'

'In a bookshop. But it was shut. I saw it in the window. And thought of you. Thought I'd buy it for you.'

The fizzing in her blood had started once more. It turned on so fast, so incredibly fast and then everything was ruined again, for so long.

'What book was it?'

'I don't remember the title. It was about one of your special subjects. One of all those things you criticize.'

He regarded her expectantly. The corners of his mouth widened disarmingly. He was not dismissing her now, but inviting her in with his dubious charm.

'Do you think I'm critical?'

'Yes.'

'Too critical?'

'Sometimes.'

'Don't you mercilessly condemn people's morality?' she said.

'Only those with power. You're critical regardless of whether people have power or not.'

'Yes, I try not to draw distinctions between people but look instead to actions, when it's actions that are relevant.'

'Pharmaceutical companies, Western regimes, top public officials and so on, they're the ones to be critical of. Not the innocent little people,' he said.

'People aren't as little as one thinks. Nor as big. The trouble with making power the basis of your judgement, rather than actions, is that virtually everyone has a let-out; they can all claim lack of power when they need to. Because everybody's powerless in the face of someone and something. Everybody's got a seam of powerlessness in them, in their perception of themselves vis-à-vis existence as a whole, which they then deploy. And that's why the world looks the way it does. Everybody's got a chink in their power, even when they know they've got power and responsibility, which they are aware they can exploit in order to understand why they have to act as they do. Morality starts with the individual. One must demand it of everybody. Those who have power are born powerless and that's the feeling that stays with them all their lives, especially at times when they are acting wrongly. Then they remember that they were bullied in the school playground and beaten by their father and realize it's all somebody else's fault this time, too.'

She wondered to what extent he was aware that she was talking about them. Presumably not at all. He looked at her, amused yet sceptical, or was it sceptically amused? She couldn't decide.

'So the starving person who steals food and money ought to study his moral philosophy a bit better?'

'Well, that person has already engaged in some moral deliberation and concluded that the best way out just then is to steal food from someone who can spare it.'

'Then I don't understand what you mean. Aren't we both saying the same thing?'

'No. According to you, everybody who is formally powerless also lacks responsibility for their actions. But in my approach, there are extra-compelling reasons for having an equal society in freedom. Because we can't expect the same actions from the hungry, the starving and those unjustly deprived of everything as we can from those who have enough, but we can demand moral insight, moral deliberation and that each individual acts in a way that causes the least harm to others.'

'What's the difference between that and what I'm saying?'

She could date the moment when she had last seen him with that intense but simultaneously unguarded expression. It was in February, just before the problems started, when they were standing among his *trompe-l'œil* sets and she expressed her appreciation of him. When he smiled at her that time there was nothing in his face but gratitude. She glimpsed it again now for a few brief seconds.

'Aren't we basically in agreement that it's power that's the deciding factor in moral responsibility, it's just that we don't agree on when one is powerless, that is, where the boundary should run?'

Ester picked up a paper serviette that he had dropped on the floor in his brief flaring of interest in the discussion, and pushed it into his trouser pocket. It was an intimate thing to do and when he did not protest in the slightest she was in raptures: the two of them belonged together in spite of everything.

'I think I actually said something different but just now I don't care what it was,' she said.

The group that had been talking about American wars of aggression had dispersed, perhaps while awaiting new ones.

She saw that Hugo's face was in thoughtful agreement and felt vindicated, and that she had been right to hold out. They were not through with each other.

He touched her arm softly, excusing himself. He had to go and talk to an old acquaintance on the other side of the room, nodded and went. Her eyes followed his back. He turned and raised a hand.

Through festively decked December streets, Ester walked home afterwards. The snow had been whirling down all day. Regular, hexagonal crystal formations, all the same, none like any other.

I'm not going to push it, she thought. Patience. Be refreshingly trustful and libertarian. Simply wait for him to get in touch. He'd probably gone to buy that book and would call her about meeting up, so he could give it to her. You couldn't pick out a book for somebody you knew to have been paralysed by yearning, someone with whom you'd moreover had congress, if you didn't mean something by it.

Don't push it now, just wait.

Christmas came, the second Christmas she had spent doing nothing but dwelling on her own feelings, her longing and her lack of appetite for life.

New Year came. She thought positively.

Twelfth Night came. She thought long-term. Don't push it. Patience. Just wait. He had chosen a book for her and you didn't do that without feeling and meaning something. He had appreciated their conversation at the Christmas party. He was still in Malmö. There was an endless succession of public holidays to get through.

She thought the next step would have to be taken with great care after feelings had been so raw. They could not rush into anything this time and they could not make a casual mess of it. This time it had to be done properly and their contact had to be fostered once it had at last been made. So it was only natural that he did not get in touch.

Fifteen days into January and a telephone as silent as the grave. She found that she was furious with him. How could he say he had picked out a book in a shop window for her if he did not want something else as well? One simply couldn't do that with their history still fresh in the memory.

The girlfriend chorus said: You aren't familiar enough with human guilt-control mechanisms, intricate, sensitive, continually duping our 'real feelings'. They're intended as a salve with dual effect, relieving the conscience of the one and the torment of the other. They only become cruel when somebody decides they should be converted into action. The words are performative, said the girlfriend chorus's academic element; one of them was writing a thesis on J. L. Austin. They are their own action; the utterance of the words of guilt control is what constitutes the guilt control. They are not intended to represent a reality outside language. That is not their intention, any more than the question 'You won't ever leave me, will you?' is about the future rather than the present.

When the girlfriend chorus persisted, Ester said it was doubtless right but she had to believe something else to be the case in order to hold out. If there were the least chance of a more positive interpretation she planned to stick with that until she was disproved.

Sixteen days into January, she called him. He did not answer but of course he could see from his display that she had rung and would therefore ring back shortly.

Two days passed. He didn't ring back.

There was nothing she could demand of him to alleviate her anguish. Talking for twenty minutes at a cocktail party did not amount to any kind of commitment. Picking out a book one intended to buy for a person one had slept with almost a year ago only meant that one was not hostile.

Why did she nonetheless consider that some kind of obligation had been placed on him? Why did she feel that her broken-heartedness was legitimate?

Ester was completely clear on the following:

Hugo Rask was not under any obligation to love her.

Being loved was not a right.

It was stuffy old honour culture that thought courting a woman or sleeping with her imposed obligations, and even more so if you came back after the first sexual act for a further two nights' union of the flesh. But that was the way she thought, even so. She saw very plainly that this was how her logic worked. Was she taking refuge in an outdated gender role particularly suited to the purpose of dealing with her disappointment? Shouldn't she rise above such fusty old notions about man's duties to the weaker sex?

She tried turning the idea round and wrote an article on the topic, which she sent to a periodical. Honour culture should not be understood as a deliberate curtailment of freedom but as the result of an observation of something entirely fundamental in human life: the fact that one has no right to run away from the wonderful thing that formed between two people who have come close to each other. Out of this sense of propriety, the old norms of behaviour had developed organically, she wrote, to prevent the suffering that results from lack of clarity and equality. Having intercourse with another person brings responsibility onto the scene, the deeper and more naked the intercourse, the more far-reaching the injunction. Honour culture had understood this and regulated it. Its aim was hardly to sentence two individuals to carry on meeting against their wills just because they had started, the way it was rigidly interpreted today, nor to keep women suppressed and supervised. Those were side effects. The crux of the matter was to induce people not to start associating in the first place if one party knew that he did not wish to be involved with the other but planned to toss her aside.

These codes for the conduct of the flesh and the emotions were not about honour, she wrote. Honour was a rationalization, after the event. It was actually an attempt to protect people from becoming mere playthings for thoughtless others. Do not hold out any prospects to the hopeful party that you know will not materialize!

Over time, the codes had been uncoupled from their original insight and had come to be falsely interpreted as demands for female virtue and decency. But the principles would have been gender-neutral if the world had been, too. They were merely a defence against what the superior position inflicts on the inferior. The holder of the superior position is the one with least to lose. And in order to implant this shield against negligence and thoughtlessness, a detailed structure of regulation was created in which everyone knew what was expected at every stage. Chastity became one component and a spontaneous result, but it was not where all this originated. Honour culture was about entirely different matters. It was instituted as a defence against people wilfully helping themselves to other people.

The article was refused.

January came to an end. People and things advanced through the winter. One weekend in February she was going to another party. She felt little enthusiasm for the event and therefore set off late. In the hall in her shoes, hat and coat she observed with some surprise that her hand was reaching out for a DVD and putting it in her bag. It was a film that had been lying about at home, one that she had borrowed from Hugo exactly a year ago after one of their long sessions at the restaurant near his studio.

Instead of walking to the stop for the part of town where the party was, her legs walked her to the stop for the number 1 bus at the corner of Fleminggatan and Sankt Eriksgatan. She would just return the DVD. She could walk on to the party from there. The film was *Gaslight*. He had said how marvellous it was and wanted her to see it so they could discuss it afterwards. She watched it twice, straight through, so she would be really well prepared with interesting reflections, but the opportunity never arose because very soon after that they went to bed and stopped talking.

She recalled the moment when their warm fingertips

met as the film exchanged hands, and the spark that it generated.

She'd have to give it back sooner or later, she thought. She needed to clean him thoroughly out of her system and her apartment. She would just hand over the film and then go. You can send it by post, the girlfriend chorus would have said, so she did not consult any of its members.

Ester got off the bus at Karlavägen, walked the short distance to Kommendörsgatan, rang the bell and was admitted by the same assistant with paint-stained trousers who had opened the door that first time she came to borrow a video artwork and he had not wanted to let her in. That was exactly fifteen months ago. Ambitious, she thought, working alone on a Saturday night. This time he recognized Ester but looked at her with a slightly uncomfortable expression that she could not read. It looked like sympathy. She did not understand why and did not think it could have anything to do with her.

'You know the way.'

He fluttered an arm in the direction of the stairs.

Hugo Rask was leaning on the bar counter in the kitchen with Eva-Stina and a glass of red at his side. Even on the stairs Ester could hear their laughter. It was Saturday and almost seven o'clock. Two colleagues staying behind at the end of the day's work, nothing peculiar about that, but Hugo remembered her name now. They did not look surprised when Ester came in, but rather blasé. They were both smoking cigarettes, which he had never done with Ester, except that time at her apartment when he had smoked five. The smoking contributed to the impression of nonchalance. Eva-Stina was not looking sideways this time, but tended more towards the condescendingly forbearing.

'Here's that film I borrowed,' said Ester, noting that her movements and speech were too hurried, giving a self-effacing, servile impression.

He took the film, seemingly not recalling that he had lent it to her or that they had talked about it, put it on a shelf and said:

'Do you want a glass of wine?'

'Well I'm on my way to a party, actually.'

Actually, thought Ester. That word again. Am I on my way to a party or not?

A glass was produced and wine was poured. The TV was on and the two of them, Eva-Stina and Hugo, talked with indolent contempt about the programme on the screen. The wine was sour and hard to drink. She didn't like wine without food, but drank some anyway. Ester, too, made some indolently contemptuous remark about the show and the current offerings on TV, feeling instantly false and disloyal to something indefinite.

'It's a good thing that there are bad programmes on television,' she corrected herself.

In unison they gave Ester a dull, quizzical look.

'Why do you mean?'

'Bad programmes with no ambitions are crucial. We

need the torrent of crap to sift the nuggets of gold out of. Unfortunately it's comparison that's the key.'

'Do you think it's because there was so much bad music that Bach wrote his?' said Eva-Stina.

'Yes, that was the only way he could see there had to be a better way to put the notes together.'

'That's not how I see it,' said Eva-Stina.

The two colleagues were about to go out for dinner. It did not seem to be an isolated occurrence or something they had decided to do on this particular evening, but part of a natural rhythm.

They all put on their outdoor clothes. Ester hastily drank up her unpalatable wine and noted the distinctive little sound of an empty glass being set down on the counter, the one she had heard so far away in Paris a thousand years ago.

They stood down in the street. It was snowing. It had snowed all winter and all day. Even here in the city it was banked up high.

'Do you want to come and eat with us?' asked Hugo.

The fact that he and Eva-Stina belonged together in some way seemed more and more evident, but Ester could not get it into her head that they could belong together in the way she had belonged with him. They were surely just particularly close colleagues; they quite often went out for driving practice, she had just learned, and laughed a lot while they were out driving, laughed at all the 'hilarious situations' they got into in the process. Eva-Stina would be taking her driving test before the summer.

If Ester had not found it absurd she would have thought they sounded like a couple in love. Instead she thought that the word hilarious was one of the worst words in the language. It was a word for people who observed that a thing was funny but didn't find it funny, yet despite this did not become ironic about it.

Her throat constricted at the thought of his having time for driving practice and hilarious situations when he had been telling her for a year that lack of time was what prevented him seeing her.

They stood on the pavement outside the entrance to his building. It was snowing. She thought: How can anyone be so stupid as to believe it's to do with time when people give time as their excuse? How can anyone be so fundamentally stupid as not to see what's obviously happening? Nothing is just sheer chance when things change. No. I'm not stupid, it's not that. I never believed time had anything to do with it. I was just trying to cope with my disappointment, weather it, get through.

Should she go for the meal? She thought it must mean, after all, that he liked her company and that the two colleagues did not have intimate dealings. You couldn't take your last woman with you when you went out for a meal with the next one. Nobody could be that tasteless.

Wasn't the question he had just posed in actual fact his way of telling Ester there wasn't anything between him and Eva-Stina, that she was just an art student who idolized him and whom he was helping with her driving test and giving career advice to?

Otherwise he would surely never have wanted all three of them to go to the restaurant together? It would be too illogical.

'But perhaps the two of you would rather be on your own?' said Ester.

'By all means come along,' said Eva-Stina.

'You've got to have dinner anyway, haven't you?' said Hugo.

'Yes. I don't feel like going to that party.'

'What party?' he said. 'Let's go. I'm quite hungry.'

Then he remembered something, turned and went up to his study. Within a minute he emerged with a slim volume.

'I got you that book I was talking about. The one I said I thought would suit you.'

He held it out to her.

'Here. A belated Christmas present.'

She looked at him, looked at the book.

The Unfortunate Consequences of Utilitarianism, it was called.

'Was this the one you saw in a shop window?'

'Yes. Or rather no. I never found that one. Bought this instead. You're interested in this sort of area, aren't you?'

'You too, I rather think.'

'Er, I suppose so. Yes, of course.'

'We did an interview on it. It caused a slight stir, as they say. Review in a national daily and all that.'

She read the back of the book.

'So did you think I ought to do some more thinking about the issues involved?'

She laughed to take the edge off her pointed question.

'Doesn't one always need to do that?'

'Yes. One always does.'

She leafed through the book and saw that it was attractively typeset.

'Thanks. How thoughtful of you.'

Ester took a surreptitious glance at the second woman, or was she the first? She looked young and unspoilt. No she didn't, in point of fact. She looked self-assured and crafty, quite calculating even. She stood calmly at his side with her hands in her jacket pockets, fur-edged hood, with an air of someone with self-evident domiciliary rights and a sense of belonging.

The snowflakes landed on their shoulders and didn't melt. On Eva-Stina's shoulders they melted instantly. Ester sensed that she ought to go home. But if she went home now she would have yet another dreadful, lonely evening. She did not intend to go to the party and in a strange way, which was actually her normal modus, she was sitting alongside what was happening and watching it, at the same time as being part of it. Thus she was far too curious about how things would develop not to accompany them.

Hugo was stamping his feet and wanted to get going. Ester kept the book open and brushed away the sprinkling of dry snowflakes on the pages.

'Why have you given me this?' she said.

'I saw the book and thought of you.'

'In what sense did you think of me?'

'I don't know. How does one think of people? Let's go and eat.'

It was apparent from his whole body and the little muscles round his eyes that he sensed something tiresome in the offing, sensed that the easy mood would not last, sensed there were critical opinions of his judgement, sensed general unpleasantness, the dreaded unpleasantness which virtually all his actions were designed to avoid.

'Perhaps you don't want it?' he said, holding out a tentative hand to take the book back.

She pressed it to her chest.

'I do want it. But I don't understand what sort of present it is.'

'No particular sort. I bought one for myself, too.'

She looked at Eva-Stina. Evidently not for her, at any rate.

'No particular sort of present. What a pity.'

'People can give each other books. Things aren't always as complicated as you think.'

'Yes they are. Everything has added levels of abstraction.

Everything that happens can be reduced to energy and matter and everything that is done has its origins in a thought, a feeling, good or bad, but everything comes from something, and everything is of some sort.'

Hugo appeared to wish he were somewhere else as he fixed his gaze on the end of the street, seeming to have grave regrets about the whole initiative, the book, the restaurant, everything. Ester knew she ought to go home, right now.

She stayed and the three of them trudged off through the snow that had fallen in the past hours, which the plough had not yet had time to deal with.

For Hugo Rask there was a table even when the restaurant was full. They bypassed the queue, there was some re-arrangement and a table for three materialized.

Ester ordered chèvre salad, Hugo entrecôte with pommes frites, and Eva-Stina had raw minced steak. The food came and they ate. The chèvre was thick and creamy, the steak juicy and tender, the raw mince completely silent.

'The food's good here,' said Hugo.

'Yes, it is,' said Ester.

'How's yours?' Hugo said to Eva-Stina.

'Sure, pretty decent,' said the second woman, or perhaps the first, who had become rather standoffish and, it appeared, ill at ease.

'I generally ask them to go easy on the garlic,' said Hugo.

'Ah no, you don't like garlic, I remember that,' said Ester.

'Not too much of it.'

'We talked about it the first time we came here for a meal together.'

'Did we?'

They might just as well have been filmed for *The Natural World*. Biology had taken over. Territory and rivals and plumage and sexual selection were in full swing. Hugo gave a quick smile, a socially acquired twitch of a muscle, yet still part of nature's game. The expressions of the second woman who might have been the first grew steadily more remote.

Ester remembered what the girlfriend chorus had once said: To be dropped for someone else is always incomprehensible, impossible to take on board. The replacement always seems preposterous. Always.

When Eva-Stina went to the toilet, Ester asked:

'So how are you?'

Hugo replied that the USA's actions were upsetting him more and more, that one had to do something, make some protest. That was what he was considering, what he as an artist could do, what his responsibility was when nobody was doing anything and the world was collapsing in front of our eyes.

He often talked like that, she noted, about nobody doing

anything, saying anything, having the guts for anything. They were all morally corrupt, bankrupt and cowardly.

'Why does no one see the injustice of society and protest against it?'

It was a wholly rhetorical question.

'Oh, surely there are a lot of people expressing opinions on that all the time?' said Ester. 'All over the media, as they say.'

'Where do you see it? To me they all seem too tied up in themselves and their own consumption.'

The plates were whisked silently away by an efficient waiter. Ester looked at Hugo. This body and this consciousness were what she had been yearning for, all day every day for almost a year and four months. She said:

'If I hadn't dropped round this evening. When were you planning to give me that book?'

'Which book?'

'The book you just gave me. The one you chose for me.'

'I don't know. I don't think about that sort of thing as much as you do. I expect I would have posted it.'

The second/first woman returned. Ester saw him smile a warm, glittering smile at her and pull out her chair, and heard him say:

'We're talking about US imperialism.'

She felt the defiance swelling like a mushroom cloud inside her.

'The Taliban are worse than all the US imperialism in the world,' she said.

'It's the West that brought the Taliban into being,' said Hugo.

'They brought themselves into being. Nobody forced them to have their ideas. But they've got them, they believe in them and they put them into practice, to the horror of the women who get in their way.'

'Is that how you think?'

'And is that how you do?' said Ester.

'They join the Taliban as a protest against some form of oppression,' said Hugo pedagogically. 'Terrorism is the only weapon of the poor.'

Ester felt suddenly weighed down and dulled by the fact that the man she loved sounded like an echo and lacked the stamina or ability to progress any further than such simplistic sloppiness.

A thought went through her head, timid as an agoraphobic it slunk along the walls of the cell, but both the thought and the anxious agoraphobic risked the walk nonetheless: this was not a person she wanted to live with. She would not be able to bear the self-sufficiency of his political morality.

'How is it,' she asked, 'that only Westerners have to answer for their actions and ideas, not other people? You and many like you divide the world into pre-determined and immutable categories of the responsible and the innocent, the active and the helpless. How can you stand yourselves and your own brutal condescension to everybody, except those you count among your own sort?'

'One simply has to have an analysis of power,' said the second woman sanctimoniously, or perhaps she was the first.

'One also has to see when the powerless wield power, and that powerlessness doesn't automatically imply that one has good sets of values,' said Ester. 'Power depends on situation. The structures recur in all situations but the people shift around in them, and behave equilaterally to each other. The same person finds him- or herself at different points in the structure in different contexts, it's not something in their skin colour, their religion or their geography.'

'Nobody's saying it's in their skin colour, religion or geography,' he said.

'No? Well then, how can you people always know in advance which party is the underdog, regardless of the question at issue?'

With suppressed irritation, Hugo signalled for the dessert menu to be brought over and said:

'My father used to say that Stalin was the only one who understood the workers' conditions.'

'He defended Stalin?'

'He understood him. Understood what he wanted to do.'

He sounded smug and looked pleased with himself.

'Do you, as well?'

'What?'

'Understand Stalin?'

He took his spectacles out of his shirt pocket and studied the choice of desserts with interest.

'But opinion is free,' said Eva-Stina. 'One has a right to think whatever one wants, surely?'

'Not if Stalin has his way. Do you defend Stalin on even a single point?' insisted Ester, turned to Hugo.

'I'm not in the same position as my father.'

'But regardless of position, your father can't defend one of the worst murderers and criminals in world history, can he?'

'That could be propaganda, at least in part.'

'This is unworthy of you, Hugo.'

'Stalin would have been good for my father and others in his position, as workers. Stalin would have furthered their interests. We haven't the right to pass judgement on this; it's a question of class interests and it was another age, things were different.'

'So workers can't rise above their own short-term interests, assuming that really was in their interests, which I dispute because reigns of terror and totalitarianism are in no one's interest, but let's assume it just for the sake of this argument. Your interests are furthered by the ideas and practices of liberalism. You make video artworks critical of society, which you'd never be allowed to do in any of the countries or political systems you applaud and defend. And yet you don't feel obliged to back up the ideas that are in your own short-term interests as a professional practitioner. In your view you have a duty, for the sake of the whole, of society and the exploited, to rise above vulgar class interests of that sort. Why don't you expect the same of your father and other workers, the ability to rise above their own self-interest? Why do you demand greater stature of yourself than of others?'

'My father was a simple labouring man. A little person who got into a tight corner.'

'It's a completely different matter, depending on whether you have power or not,' said Eva-Stina, which sounded a bit repetitive this time.

'So workers can't make ethical assessments for any other reason than their own profit?' said Ester. 'Can't think of anything but themselves and their interests? Can't pay regard to the whole, or to the lives of others?'

Hugo inserted a toothpick between two of his teeth and turned towards Eva-Stina to ask what she wanted for dessert. Sorbet, came the answer. Hugo wanted chocolate fondant. So did Ester but with such tension between them she could not have the same as him and had to settle for panna cotta.

'Mayakovsky was in favour of the Soviet state,' said Hugo once they had ordered. 'Read "My Soviet Passport". "Envy me – I happen to be a citizen of the Soviet Union".'

'Let's hope he wouldn't have written that if he'd known what we know.'

Hugo Rask cast a longing look out into the winter night, where the falling snow could be clearly seen under the street lights. Big, round flakes. For a few seconds,

Ester was seized by the feeling of having had the chance to resume a relationship with him but having thrown it away by coming across as overbearing, sharp-tongued and polemical.

Now he'll choose her instead of me, she thought. This was the moment I lost him and crushed the fragile shoot that had started to re-grow. Taking us both out to dinner was a test, and here and now he realized definitively that he didn't want me. His final doubts, which he wanted to examine one last time tonight, evaporated right here.

Her face flushing, she said:

'Well naturally, it all depends on one's perspective.'

How hideously unnecessary to get into a discussion of Stalin and the Taliban.

She regretted doing it. She didn't regret doing it.

She still couldn't live with someone who thought in catchphrases and kept to the sleek outer layer of activism so as never to have to descend to the labyrinth of investigation.

The waitress was approaching with more food and his smile broke out like fire from green timber. They quickly ate their desserts and then he produced his wallet like some rich businessman in a cartoon and paid for all three of them.

'You needn't,' said Ester.

'Don't mention it.'

He closed his wallet with a bang so the weight of responsibility was clearly audible and got to his feet to tower over his two followers. They went up Nybrogatan, three abreast, crossed the square to Sibyllegatan and continued towards Kommendörsgatan. The snow fell.

The two colleagues were returning to their workplace while Ester would walk on to her bus stop. They stopped outside to say goodbye.

'Thank you for the book and the dinner,' said Ester.

'Hope you find it useful.'

'I'm sure I will.'

He raised his arm in a wave.

'Best of luck, then,' he said.

She saw the two of them enter his door. Then she walked along the pavement as she had done so many times before. How many pavements must a person walk down, before she gives up?

'Best of luck, then,' she thought, a phrase with all the qualities of a murder weapon. *People are created to torment one another*. She had underlined that sentence when she read *The Idiot* not long before.

She halted in mid-step and stood still. She saw all at once with absolute clarity what she must do. And she must do it now. Far too much remained unresolved. This evening was the chance to talk it through. Something had to happen this evening. She went back to the building. He owed her a proper conversation.

The lights were still on in the studio. Ester could wait. She was a little elated by the thought that they could finally talk to each other about everything there'd been and why it had turned out the way it did, and by the prospect of what could happen then, where a frank conversation might lead in the middle of the night and with alcohol in their bodies.

She walked round the block. When she got back they would undoubtedly have finished in there. When she got back the lights would be off and the place in darkness.

When she got back a window had been opened wide and she could hear a game of table tennis in progress.

They were laughing to each other in that polite way you do when you want to like somebody but there's a vacuum in between, when you feel goodwill but no sense of affinity, when you want to show that you're having fun together but are not on your own ground and aren't finding the chosen activity particularly edifying. You take part and show pleasure for the other person's sake. When everything's a bit artificial. That was the way they were laughing.

She had laughed like that herself sometimes. But never with him. With him she had never played or pretended or felt uncomfortable. Once he told her he had never shared conversations with anyone as he had with her. Talking was her aphrodisiac, the only one she knew and had mastered. Through conversation she could knock down anyone who shared her appetite for verbal sparring and the exchange of ideas. The conversations between her and Hugo had been erotically charged, never-ending and infinitely rewarding – but apparently not indispensable. People could clearly live without interesting conversations. Their primary need was not verbal-erotic intercourse but absence of inconvenience. That always took priority over the desire for substance and meaning. They bought this freedom from bother at the price of mild ennui.

Ester Nilsson stood on the pavement in Kommendörs-gatan with frozen feet and thought that unusually lively activities seemed to be laid on for those who worked there. She waited another hour in her coat of hopelessly inade-quate thickness. Then the lights finally went out and the premises were dark except for a faint gleam from a back room. She waited another five minutes. Then she went through the entrance, across the courtyard and up the stairs to his flat.

The smell of the stairwell was as she remembered it, old dust and cold stone. The smell would have been painful, as recollections are, but her sense of expectation was stronger. The door to his flat stood ajar. She knocked.

'Yes?' came his voice, friendly and expectant.

She took a step into the hall. How she had longed for this, to talk everything over with him properly, undis-turbed, in his home, when neither of them was on their way somewhere else.

She heard him coming to meet her, walking from the kitchen, rounding the corner. Now she saw him, his shining, full-moon face that generally also bore a look of slight doubt and introspection.

Ester started to say something. She had practised it while she was stamping her feet out in the street. It ran: I thought we could have a little talk now, seeing how nice it was this evening. We've never had the chance to talk properly about what happened and where we actually stand and what we're going to do with the beautiful thing we built between us.

That was what she had worked out that she would say.

This perpetual talk that the jilted party feels obliged to engage in. This perpetual talk. The jilter never feels the need to talk.

She, if anyone, should have known that the one walking away feels no pain; the one walking away does not need to talk because they have nothing to talk about. The one leaving is through with it. It's the one left behind who needs to talk for an eternity. And all that this talk boils down to is repeated attempts to tell the other person he's made a mistake. That if only he realized the true nature of things he would not make the choice he has, but would love her. The talk is nothing to do with gaining clarity, as the talker claims, and everything to do with convincing and inducing.

There's no point talking. Honest answers are never forthcoming, to show consideration. One betrays and is betrayed and there's nothing to talk about because there are no obligations when the will is not to hand. What is done out of compassion is worth little if the other party hopes it is done out of love.

Ester did not have time to say what she had planned, but she made a start:

'I thought we could . . .'

Then she registered the expression on his face. It was the expression of someone who has just swallowed a snake.

Hugo was expecting someone. But not her. The words that came out of his mouth were tactless with panic and dismay, or whatever it was he was now feeling.

'Someone else . . . is coming . . . Eva-Stina's . . . coming.'

Ester slammed the door and ran down the stairs, all but sliding down the banisters to avoid a meeting in the stairwell with the second woman, who was the first. She must still be in the studio, seeing to something. Perhaps she was putting the final touch of paint to a set piece.

Definitive answers are easier to deal with than diffuse ones. This is to do with Hope and its nature. Hope is a parasite on the human body, which lives in full-scale symbiosis with the human heart. It is not enough to put it in a strait-jacket and lock it up in dark corners. Starvation rations do not help either; a parasite cannot be put on a diet of bread and water. The supply of nourishment must be completely cut off. If Hope can find oxygen, it will. There can be oxygen in a poorly directed adjective, a rash adverb, a compensatory sympathetic gesture, a bodily movement, a smile, a gleam in an eye. The hopeful party will choose to remain oblivious to the fact that empathy is a mechanical force. The indifferent party automatically shows care, for self-protection and to shield the person in distress.

Hope has to be starved to death if it is not to beguile and bedazzle its host. Hope can only be killed by the brutality of clarity. Hope is cruel because it binds and entraps.

When the parasite Hope is taken from its carrier the Host, the carrier either dies or is set free.

Hope and its symbiosis, it must be said, do not believe

in a change in the innermost will of the beloved. The hope that inhabits the human heart believes that this will is already present; that the beloved really – actually – wants what he pretends not to want, or does not want what he pretends to want, but has been misled by the evil world around him into wanting; in short, that things are not as they seem. That the tiny glimpse of something else is the truth.

That is what Hope is.

When Ester got home that night she went through her normal pre-bedtime routine. It was a year since Hugo had come round for dinner. They had eaten a reddish dish and he had gone to the window once an hour to smoke. In a week's time she would have endured a year of suffering. It would intensify and become more concentrated for a few days now, but it was purer and less unclear.

There was nothing left to understand.

picador.com

blog
videos
interviews
extracts